JOSHUA

THE BURNETT BRIDES
BOOK EIGHT

SYLVIA MCDANIEL

Spend Christmas with the Burnetts—where love, family, and a meddling ghost make the holidays unforgettable.

Joshua Burnett is the next target on his ghostly great-great-great-great-grandmother's matchmaking list. But he's hiding secrets—secrets even she doesn't know. His womanizing ways may have a deeper reason, but nothing could have prepared him for the biggest surprise of his life: a baby daughter he never knew existed.

Kayla Scott has lost everything she once dreamed of. When she applies for a nanny position with the Burnett family, she expects a fresh start—but not the unexpected twist of caring for Joshua's newborn.

Forced together by circumstance, Kayla and Joshua's clashing worlds spark emotions neither of them are ready for. Kayla swore she'd never let herself hope again, and Joshua isn't even sure he wants to be a father. But with a determined ghost meddling in their lives, they may have no choice but to confront their pasts—and their hearts—before Christmas morning arrives.

Can love find a way, even when its biggest obstacles are the ones they never saw coming?

CHAPTER 1

*J*oshua Burnett liked women. Lots of women. And dating more than one at a time was never out of the question. The more the merrier. Date them, bed them, and then tell them good-bye. That was his motto and he lived by it religiously.

He rolled over in bed next to his latest conquest, Marcy Anderson. They'd been sleeping together for the last month, and he liked how it was all about the sex. No commitments, no promises of forever, nothing but a good time. And Marcy was the one who set the rules, not him.

But they fit very well within his own set of regulations.

Lying in bed, he glanced at her. "We're still going to the rodeo tonight?"

"Yes," she said, rising from the bed naked.

He liked her body, and he liked the way she enjoyed partying late into the night, having sex until dawn, sleeping until noon, and then afternoon sex. Every weekend, they stayed at either his place or hers.

She'd let him know right up front that she wasn't inter-ested in marriage or anything permanent and that was all he needed to hear. When the time came and he was finished with her, he'd say good-bye.

"Guess we better get up and get ready to go," he said, throwing his feet over the side of the bed. It was the Friday after Thanksgiving and instead of fighting crowds at the mall, they had spent the day in bed.

He jumped into the shower and she joined him there.

"We're invited to go out with the bull riders after the rodeo," she said, washing his back.

"Sounds like fun," he said, thinking how those men lived life on the edge and partied like it was their last night.

And it could be.

After stepping out of the shower, he pulled on a fresh pair of jeans, tucked one of his good shirts into his pants, and slipped on his boots.

Turning, he watched Marcy spray her hair, making certain the curls stayed in place. Her makeup was spotless and he knew he'd be the envy of every cowboy at the rodeo tonight.

She turned and smiled.

"Ready?"

"Yes," he said. They started toward the garage. The sound of knocking on his front door had him frowning.

"Let me get that and then we'll go." It was probably one of the workers there to tell him something about the cattle.

After walking into his living area, he opened the front door, and his eyes widened.

An old girlfriend from over a year ago, Skylar Beal, stood

in front of him, looking gorgeous, her blonde hair longer than ever, holding a baby.

"Skylar," he said, surprised. She hardly seemed like the motherly type. "What are you doing here?"

She thrust the baby into his arms and he had no choice but to accept the child or let it drop to the ground.

"What the hell?"

Her brown eyes flashed with determination and she stepped back far enough away he couldn't give her the baby back.

"It's your turn. I haven't gone out and had fun in ages, Josh. I've been pregnant then dealing with Mia. Now it's my turn for some fun. You can watch her for the weekend."

The woman had completely lost it. "I'm not watching your kid. Why would I?"

The smirk he had hated from the day he met her filled her face. "She's yours, hotshot. Deal with it. I had to."

Terror filled his chest and his heart raced like a formula one driver's car nearing the concrete wall.

"What? This baby isn't mine," he yelled.

Two big sapphire eyes popped open and the baby's bottom lip trembled before she belted out a cry.

"Now you've done it," Skylar said, dropping a bag on the ground at his feet. "Her formula, diapers, everything you'll need is here in this bag. I'll be back late Sunday to pick her up. Have a great weekend getting to know your daughter Mia."

Turning around in her cowboy boots, she all but ran down the stairs and jumped into her Corvette. The engine roared to life and she backed out of his drive, spinning gravel as she took off.

Shocked, he stared down at the baby in his arms. This child was his? No...

What the hell was he going to do? He didn't know anything about taking care of babies. What kind of mother just ran off and left her child with an amateur?

Marcy came up behind him. "Are you ready?" Her eyes widened with concern. "Where did the baby come from?"

"Skylar just dropped her off. Said she was mine." He wasn't certain he believed her, but what was he going to do? Her mother was gone.

The baby cried louder, and with disbelief, Joshua picked up the diaper bag, brought it into the house, and closed the door.

Marcy shook her head. "Ew. I don't do screaming babies or men with kids. It's been fun, Josh. Call me if you get this straightened out. But not if you have a kid. Have a good night. I'm going to the rodeo."

He could only watch as she picked up her purse and overnight bag and walked out the door. And just like that, she was out of his life. Probably forever.

Normally, he ended the relationship, not the other way around. He shrugged. "Oh, well. You ended that, Mia."

While Marcy was a beautiful woman, they were a dime a dozen down at the club. Soon he'd find another.

"Women," he said, gazing down at the child. "This is why I'll never marry. What am I going to do with you? Do you like sports? Football? How about cartoons? What is going to make you happy?"

The baby's bottom lip trembled and those eyes that he suddenly feared gazed at him. They were the same damn color as most of the Burnett men – startling blue eyes that gave them away.

How in the hell had Skylar had his child without telling him she was pregnant? No, she was just using him and she'd be lucky if he didn't call Child Protective Services on her.

But then he glanced down and gazed at the crying baby. What if she was his? And if his family learned about her, he would be in dog shit creek without a boat.

Opening the diaper bag, he glanced through the contents, not knowing what everything was for. Skylar hadn't given him instructions on what to do.

How could he keep this child through Sunday? Today was Friday. That would be two whole days.

"What do you need?" he asked the little girl who couldn't be more than three months old. "A clean diaper? A bottle? Tell me. A million dollars? Hell, I'd give you the ranch right now to keep you from crying."

Where was she going to sleep? He didn't have a crib.

He laid her on the carpet and then he went into the closet and came back with a fluffy blanket. Grabbing a baby blanket out of her bag, he laid a large quilt and then laid the child on her blanket.

"She said your name is Mia. Let's start with changing your diaper. Maybe that would make you stop crying." He took out a plastic-lined diaper from the bag.

He unsnapped the outfit she had on and pulled the wet diaper free.

"Can you please not poop until your mother returns," he told her. "My weak stomach won't be able to handle it, and where would I put the nasty diaper? It's not like we have trash pickup every day out here on the ranch. Just hold your poop."

The baby farted as if to reply *not happening.*

Those blue eyes gazed at him and he could see she wasn't certain about him. Lifting her legs, he slid the fresh diaper beneath her and then pulled the tabs hoping it was tight enough. At least he didn't get baby pee on him.

That would be gross.

"It would help if you could tell me if I was doing this right. You'll cry if I get it too tight. You'll wet on me if I get it too loose. I'm not cut out to be a babysitter or even a father. This is why I don't have children."

The baby stopped crying and gazed at him.

"Now what do we do?" he asked. "You're too young to drink, but I sure could use a whiskey right now."

She kicked her legs and he sat back on his heels and stared at her.

Was Mia his daughter? Was he a father?

"Damn, your mother has some questions to answer when she gets back here. In fact, I'm going to call her right now."

He picked up his phone and dialed Skylar's cell number which he still had in his contacts, miraculously.

"You have reached Skylar Beal. Joshua, you're her father, deal with her. I'm on my way to a fabulous shopping trip that will end with a party I'm attending on Saturday night. Sex for the first time in months. Don't call me again unless it's an emergency."

Click.

She'd changed her voice message just for him. Bitch.

Glancing down at the baby, he groaned. "Your mother

comes from one of the richest families in Texas, why didn't she hire a nanny? Was this her way of getting revenge?"

The baby kicked her feet and then blew him a raspberry and his heart melted a little. She was cute.

But he didn't want marriage. He didn't want kids. He didn't want commitment. As a boy, he'd witnessed enough to make him positive he'd never get married.

Give him a woman like Marcy who only wanted mutual, gratifying sex and he was happy.

Suddenly the baby let out a squeal that quickly turned to tears.

"What's wrong? What do you need?"

Running his hand through his hair, he shook his head. Sure he'd had brothers, but they had been close together. He'd never been around babies much. He knew nothing.

Crying, she looked up at him, and he wanted to jump in his truck and race after her mother. But there was no way his truck could catch her Corvette.

He was a player, not a father, and he had no idea what babies needed. And he hated her crying because it made him feel like he was failing her.

What the hell was he going to do?

CHAPTER 2

A year ago, Kayla Scott was making lots of money and at the top of her game in the corporate world. One stupid mistake had her out on the streets, brokenhearted and looking for a job.

At the time, she had no intention of becoming a nanny. With a solid education in advertising and a good career at a prestigious firm, becoming a nanny was out of the question. But…life happened.

After losing everything, she was beginning to rebuild her life. A job as a nanny last year had seemed like the perfect thing—and it was. Until the family relocated to New Zealand and she'd been forced to take short-term jobs until the agency pointed her in this direction.

Lately, she'd been toying with the idea of starting her own online company where she could work from home and also enjoy being a nanny. With a steady income from her nanny position, she would be free to get her online company off the ground without going through her savings.

To hell with Frantz Marketing Company. They fired their best salesperson, and now she would give them a run for their money. But first, she had to interview for her new position and hope and pray she was hired.

Tonight, she would be launching her new company and stealing as many of her old customers from the marketing firm that had done her wrong.

Driving up the road, she stopped at the guard house.

"Good morning," she said. "I'm here to meet with Samantha and Emily Burnett."

"Yes, ma'am. Follow the road past the clubhouse. I'm phoning them now to let them know you're here. They will be standing outside waiting for you."

"Thank you," she said as she put the car in drive. The sound of its roar always gave her pleasure. It was her last remaining luxury, and she'd been loathed to part with the car.

The dude ranch was huge and she noted the guest quarters as she drove past them. On one side were luxury homes and on the other were the guest cottages. In the distance stood a large barn.

Sunday was the only day they could interview her and she agreed to drive out here. The agency had given them a detailed background check on her. That was fine, she had nothing to hide. Leaving the corporate world had not been her choice, but for her sanity, it had been the right decision at the time.

As much as she loved that job, corporate politics had gotten her fired. Sleeping with the boss's son was never a good idea. Even when he promised her they were going to marry.

Even when he told his daddy that she was the right woman for him.

Two women stepped out of a large house and waved at her.

She pulled her Aston Martin to the curb and parked. Taking a deep breath, she stepped out of the vehicle and smiled at the women.

Time to put her sales tactics to work. She needed this job.

"Good morning," she said. "I'm Kayla Scott."

The two women glanced at one another.

"You're here for the job?" the blonde asked.

"Yes," she said, smiling, wondering why they were surprised.

"I'm Emily and this is Samantha Burnett."

The women were very pregnant and Samantha looked to be due in the next two months. But Kayla needed a job now. Not in the future.

With a sigh, she shook each woman's hand. Driving out here, she thought this seemed like the perfect position. Two babies and living on a ranch in the middle of nowhere. She would have time to set up her business.

"Follow us," Samantha said as she led them into the house.

"Would you like some tea or coffee?"

"No, thanks," she said, knowing that would only make her even more nervous. And though this might not be the job for her, she would still interview. Maybe it would be a future job she could consider.

"When are you due?" she asked, taking a seat on a couch Emily pointed her to.

"The end of February," Emily said.

"I'm due the first of February," Samantha replied as the two women sank down across from her.

For a moment, the two women stared.

"You don't look like a nanny," Samantha said.

She smiled. That was what everyone said. But getting out of the corporate world had been good for her. And now she only wanted to do that part-time.

"Your resume said you were once a sales executive for a big marketing firm in Dallas," Emily said.

There was always the question of how much she should tell the families about her past. She never knew what would scare them or make them question her judgment.

"It was for the best that I left the corporate world," she said. "I'm much happier taking care of little ones. The only reason I left the last nanny position was because the family moved to New Zealand."

Samantha was the one she could see questioning her decision. "I, too, left a powerful corporate job. What made you leave?"

This was the question she hated to answer, but she would.

"The boss's son and I were involved and when he ended it abruptly, they fired me. But it was for the best. I needed a break from the politics and office gossip."

She refused to tell them why he ended it. That was personal and not even the agency knew. That was her own private hell she didn't talk about.

Samantha nodded.

"What made you decide to become a nanny?" Emily asked. "It seems like such a jump to go from an executive to a nanny."

11

This was also a difficult question to answer because she refused to tell everyone her reason.

"I'm twenty-seven years old and I doubt that I will ever have children of my own, so I decided to take care of other people's children. This way, I'm involved, but you as their parents have to complete their training and raising. I just watch over them and keep them safe when you're not available. Of course, I also get to love on them and enjoy their sweetness."

The two women glanced at one another.

"I work in the kitchen from early in the morning until that evening," Emily said. "Would that be a problem?"

"Oh, no," she said, knowing she could work on her dream at night.

"I won't need your help as much," Samantha said. "I'm writing a book and need about four hours a day to put some words on the page."

"What's the book about?" she asked.

"Ghost hunters," she said. "I had a television show on ghost hunting."

"That's unique." She wondered how one did a show on ghosts. Just then, two cowboys walked into the room, shedding their coats, and putting their hats on a rack in the hallway. This must've been their husbands.

"Hi," a dark-haired man said. "I'm Travis Burnett. I'm married to Samantha."

Another man walked in. He was quieter. "Tanner Burnett," he said as he glanced at his wife. "You doing all right?"

She smiled. "I'm fine. She's kicking like crazy this morning, but I'm used to it."

"He's going to be a fine bull rider," the man said, smiling at his wife.

The woman shook her head. "Two months and we'll see who is right."

Kayla liked the way the two of them bantered about the sex of the child. She liked happy homes and when the parents told her their expectations.

"If you hire me, what are you looking for in a nanny?"

The two couples glanced at one another.

"Someone to give my wife a break, so she can spend more time with me," Tanner said.

"Someone to watch our little munchkin until I can take care of her," Emily said.

"I'll be honest with you. I don't want a nanny. I want my wife to be the mother to our children. It would be nice to eventually use you to get away for an evening. But that's all," Tucker said.

Samantha didn't seem to take offense. "You know, I've told you that I want to continue working. All I need are a couple of hours a day. The rest of the time, I'll be here being a mother to our son."

"Daughter," Travis said as he reached down and kissed her on the head.

"If you offer me the job, when would you expect me to start?"

"Probably not until April," Emily said. "I'm taking the first six weeks off to spend with our newborn."

That was not going to work well for her at all. She needed a job now.

Just then the door burst open and a man carrying a screaming baby came rushing in.

"Help. I need help," the handsome man cried, his face desperate.

CHAPTER 3

*J*oshua's head was pounding. He'd barely slept the last two nights and he was at his wits' end.

He'd fed the baby, changed her, and walked the floors trying to get her to stop crying. But nothing helped. Every time he got her to sleep and then laid her down, she started crying again.

He'd called, texted, and left Skylar a hundred messages, but the woman was ignoring him. Typical Skylar. He wondered if she was even worthy of being a mother to this child.

Finally he feared the baby must be sick or in pain or something that he had no control over, so he picked her up and ran to his cousin Tanner's house. Emily and Samantha were both pregnant. Surely one of them could help him get her to stop crying before he lost his mind.

When he ran through the door, he was stunned to see a beautiful blonde woman sitting on the couch. If he hadn't been so distressed, he would have tried to make a move on her, but right now, Mia was his only focus.

Her lungs were in fine shape, but he was a nervous wreck.

The people in the house all stared at him, surprised expressions on their faces. He must look crazy. For the last two days, he hadn't showered. He'd barely brushed his teeth. All he'd done was try to make this baby happy.

She'd even cried during the Dallas Cowboys game. And he'd wanted to bawl with her.

"I can't get her to stop crying," he said. "I've done everything I know to do. I've changed her, given her a bottle, and nothing makes her happy. She's thrown up on me twice."

He smelled of spoiled baby burp. If this was a typical day with a baby, why would anyone want children?

The beautiful woman he didn't know stood and walked over to him. "May I?"

Needing a break, he placed Mia in her arms, hoping this woman had some magic trick that would make the baby stop crying.

She began to rock the infant and made soothing noises between asking Joshua questions.

"How old is she?"

"I don't know. Maybe three months?"

"Where is her mother?"

Shaking his head, he all but growled. "In Dallas, shopping and going to a party. She should be back later today."

"What are you doing with her?" Travis asked. "You are the least likely person I would leave a child with."

"I know," he said.

Joshua knew that when he said the words, there would be a stunned reaction. As much as he didn't want to admit to it, he had to tell them the truth.

"Skylar says she's mine, but I don't know that for certain," he said. "She dropped her off and told me it was my turn to watch her for a while."

The men in the room grinned at him and he could see the women trying not to laugh. Really? They thought it was funny that he'd just learned he was a possible father and he knew nothing about children.

"You said you fed her, right? What did you give her?"

"The bottles that were in the bag," he said. "But she didn't like them."

The woman holding Mia frowned. "Did you warm them up?"

What was she talking about? "No, I just took them from the refrigerator. When I put them in her mouth, she would cry and scream."

Emily and Samantha snickered.

"You need to warm them," the woman said. "Babies want their milk warm or room temperature. The same temperature as if they were being breastfed."

Why hadn't he thought of that? Because he was a bachelor.

He wasn't meant to be a father. They all stared at him like he was the dumbest human being on the planet, but he'd never been around infants. He didn't know they liked their milk hot.

Reaching into the bag, he pulled a bottle out.

Kayla put her finger in the baby's mouth and she sucked on it. "She's hungry. Would one of you please warm the bottle for me?"

Emily took the bottle from Josh, shaking her head at him. "Why didn't you come over sooner?"

"Because I hoped I could speak to Skylar and confirm Mia is mine before everyone learned of her."

In a moment, Emily returned. The couples watched as Kayla tested the heat of the bottle before she gave it to the little girl.

The baby sighed and began to moan with pleasure. Her mouth made little sucking noises. She had not done that with him.

"Poor baby; she's hungry," she said, gazing down at the little girl. After several slurps, she lifted the child to her shoulder where Mia burped a loud healthy sound and then resumed eating.

When the baby finished, she was sound asleep, her arm slung over her head, relaxed.

Joshua shook his head. If only he'd known, his life would not have been a living hell for two days and this poor child would not have suffered.

In many ways, he felt bad.

"You're hired," Travis said, gazing at Kayla with amazement.

"Oh no," Josh said. "You can have her when Skylar arrives to pick up Mia. Until then, she's working for me. Don't even think of trying to keep her."

The woman glanced up at him and shook her head. "What makes you think I want to work for you?"

"I'll pay you double whatever they offered," Joshua said. "It will only be until tonight or until Skylar arrives. Skylar is her mother," he said.

The couples all glanced at Kayla.

"We don't need you just yet," Samantha said.

"And Joshua and Mia do," Emily replied.

The woman glanced down at the sleeping baby in her arms. For the first time in days, the child slept peacefully. Guilt filled Josh at how he'd starved her because of his lack of knowledge. He needed this woman, desperately.

"I'm Joshua Burnett, by the way," he said. "And you're holding Mia."

"Kayla Scott," she said quietly.

She glanced up at him. "I'll stay and help you. You said her mother was returning tonight?"

"Yes," he said, hoping Skylar was for once in her life on time, but fearing it would be late or even tomorrow before he saw her. "Thank you. And I know Mia thanks you."

He glanced up from the woman and saw his cousins laughing at him.

"Just wait. Your turn is coming," he told them. "And at least you know you've got a baby coming. I knew nothing. Nothing like having a baby shoved into your arms and told she's yours. Deal with it."

A frown crossed Travis's face. "You need to do a DNA test right away. Insist on one. I don't know Skylar, but you can't be too trusting."

What no one knew was that Skylar's family was probably wealthier than the Burnetts, but they were a strange group. In fact, Skylar had been raised by nannies. She had seldom seen her jet-setting parents. And then when she went away to college, the partying began. When they dated, she was wild and free and often partying to the extreme. And now she had a child that she claimed was his.

He glanced down at Mia. What kind of father would he be to this little girl, who deep in his gut, he knew was his?

"Let's go," he said, glancing at Kayla.

The woman was gorgeous, and now they would spend hours in his house, waiting on Skylar to return for Mia. Hours of being close, and yet she was taking care of his daughter.

As soon as they returned to the house, he would text Skylar and tell her time to come home. Now.

Plus, he had to cancel his date for tonight. With a sigh, he realized just how much children interfered in their parents' lives. And she was only three months old.

CHAPTER 4

*T*he interview had taken an unexpected turn. One she never anticipated. But the cries of the sweet little girl she held could not be ignored. They had reached into her heart and tugged on the pain she kept hidden there.

The cry of the child could not be disregarded and she felt drawn to the baby. She needed her and Kayla needed the comfort of the infant.

Each one was helping the other in a way only they understood.

As they walked across the yard, she knew she could not become attached to this child because she wouldn't be here long. Fewer than twenty-four hours.

"What were they going to pay you?"

"We hadn't gotten that far. And since this is a short job, I'll expect five hundred dollars."

Yes, it was a lot, but that would tide her over until she got her next nanny position. Or at least, she hoped it would.

"Is that Aston Martin your car?" he asked. "Being a nanny seems to pay well."

The car had been the only luxury she'd retained from her lavish lifestyle. Gone were the expensive apartment, the luxurious wardrobe, and the weekly spa treatments. Now she lived a modest life with a pricey car.

"I bought that with the bonus money I made when I worked for a corporation," she said. She doubted she would ever earn that kind of money again.

It was her reminder about the company that had done her wrong. Her vow to return to the comfortable status she once held.

"Must have been a hell of a bonus," he said.

"It was," she replied.

Since he'd already hired her, she wasn't divulging any of her private information. That was on a need-to-know basis, and he didn't need to know. She'd been fired before and lived through it, and she could be again.

When they walked into the house, she saw where he had been keeping the baby. She strolled over and laid the child on the blanket. Then she changed the tiny diaper. The poor baby made sweet little noises but went right back to sleep.

The little one was sated and resting.

Joshua was on his phone texting someone, probably the child's mother.

"She needs to get back here," he said to himself. "I kept her for the weekend, but she promised me she'd be back today."

Then he dialed a number and walked into the kitchen area. Only problem was that she could still hear him.

"Sugar, I'm sorry, but I can't make it tonight. No, no there is not another woman. No, it's not a game. Darling, you know you're important to me. I've got to work tonight."

The man was lying. The only work tonight was taking care of Mia.

"Darling, I'll make it up to you. I promise. We'll go out next week, and you know what I do to you," he said low.

After many more apologizes and promises to the woman on the line, he hung up and walked into the living area.

Kayla sat on the couch near the baby who was sleeping soundly now that she was fed and had a clean diaper.

"What is her name?" she asked, disliking how he'd treated the woman on the phone.

"Whose name?"

"The woman you were speaking to. Usually when a man calls her *darling* and *sugar* that means he doesn't remember her name."

The man gave her a sly grin and shook his head.

"Oh, I know her name. It's Patty. And I was really looking forward to spending time with her. But I can't. Not with this situation here. I have to speak to Skylar."

At least he recognized that he needed to be here for his daughter. That was points in his favor. Not many, but still a few she wouldn't have given him.

"How could you not know you had a daughter?"

The man sighed. "Her mother is the daughter of a rich oil billionaire. Her father and mother travel the world and they didn't raise their daughter. Her nanny took care of her. When Skylar grew up, she liked to party.

"We met over a year ago and dated for about six weeks before I ended it. That was the last time I saw her until she showed up at my door Friday evening. I didn't know she was pregnant. I didn't know this child could be mine until Skylar laughed and told me I needed to get to know my daughter. Even now, I'm not certain."

The man was obviously a player. Her least favorite kind of man. The type who had burned her badly in the past, and now she was here taking care of his baby.

But he didn't matter. The child was all that was important to her. Joshua could continue his hound-dogging ways because she avoided men like him at all costs. Once burned, twice shy, even though he was handsome as sin.

Even though his jeans fit tight and clung to his well-shaped derriere like a wet T-shirt.

And those muscles of his were rippled and firm and looked hard as a rock. But it was the blue eyes that would cause a woman to melt. Just one glance with the long dark lashes could set panties a flame. And Mia had that same color.

It was all she could do not to say *have you heard of birth control*? But then again, sometimes it just didn't work. Sometimes even protection didn't stop a pregnancy.

"Now you can no longer go back to not knowing," she said.

Shaking his head, he stared at the baby lying on the blanket. "I always use protection. Always."

What most men didn't understand was that birth control was not one hundred percent foolproof. Ever.

"Tomorrow I'm going to contact my lawyer and ask how I get a DNA test done. I'm still not convinced she's mine."

Leaning back like he was done talking about Mia, he turned on the game and she glanced down at the baby to see if she had awakened. But the child slept on. This was going to be the easiest five hundred dollars she'd ever made.

Sitting there watching Sunday night football, she kept glancing at the child, wanting to pick her up and hold her. To feel her in her arms. But that wouldn't be a good idea. It was for one night. One night only.

The smell of a dirty diaper reached her nose. Suddenly, the baby made quiet little farting noises.

"Oh no," Joshua said. "That child has the stinkiest poop."

"Most babies do," she said.

The child's eyes opened wide and she blew a raspberry and kicked her feet.

Kayla sank onto the blanket and smiled at the baby. "Good evening, sunshine. I bet you're ready for a clean diaper."

The little girl cooed and it was the sweetest sound.

Kayla glanced at Joshua, who refused to look at his child. His eyes were firmly on the television, on the game where big men grunted and groaned as they tried to stop the other team from advancing with the ball.

There was so much more to life than watching television. Lifting the baby's legs, she cleaned her up with a wet wipe.

"That's what those are for," Joshua said. "I didn't know why she sent me those. I thought they were hand sanitizer."

The man was clueless when it came to babies and the thought of him spending the last two days alone with her sent a trickle of fear down her spine.

"They keep her clean between baths," Kayla said, pulling on a new diaper. "You're getting low on diapers. I hope you have enough to last until her mother arrives."

He glanced at his watch. "It's getting close to eight. I would have thought she would be here before now. I'm going to call her."

He dialed the number on his phone and there was no answer. Only her voice message that said the box was full.

"What if she doesn't come back tonight?" Kayla asked, thinking that this woman was truly not responsible. This beautiful baby didn't stand a chance with a mother that dropped her off with a man who knew nothing about how to take care of a child.

His brows drew together in a frown. And she could see that he was concerned.

"I'll pay you extra to stay," he said. "I can't be trusted with her alone. She needs someone who knows what they're doing."

That was for certain. But she hadn't brought a change of clothes. Nothing.

"I have a supply of extra toothbrushes."

She just bet he did. He probably even had a change of clothes for her if she wanted one.

Picking the baby up, the little one cooed at her and she knew she couldn't leave her. Not now. Not when her mother hadn't returned.

"I'll stay," she said. "Do you have a spare bedroom, I can sleep in?"

"Yes," he said. "We can move the baby quilt in there."

Glancing down at the baby, she wondered where the child's mother was. Why had she not come as promised to pick her up this evening? How irresponsible was that?

The baby gurgled happily and Kayla wished she had a baby toy for her, but she'd looked through the bag and found nothing. So she held her, smiling and cooing at her who swung her arms up and blew a raspberry.

At midnight, she picked up the sleeping child and carried her into the spare bedroom. Joshua moved the quilt and she laid the child down and then she covered her with another baby blanket.

When she stood, Joshua was staring down at her.

"She's been a different baby since you arrived," he said. "She's happy and no longer screaming and crying."

That was an easy explanation. "She's full, she's warm, and now she can sleep all night," Kayla said, glancing at the man who even now looked guilty.

"I'm not a good father. Why Skylar left her with me, I don't understand. And why she didn't pick her up is baffling. I'm afraid for Mia's safety. Maybe tomorrow I should call Child Protective Services."

"Not if you think there's a chance she's yours," Kayla said, knowing from firsthand experience what that felt like. "Let's wait and see what tomorrow brings."

"I have an extra-large T-shirt you can sleep in," he said, gazing at her sheepishly.

She couldn't help but wonder how many other women he'd offered the shirt to. But she didn't want to sleep nude and she couldn't sleep comfortably in her clothes.

"Thank you," she replied.

A few minutes later, he returned and handed her the T-shirt. It was large, clean, and would feel comfortable for tonight. Tomorrow she would be leaving.

Her chest ached at the thought of leaving this baby behind.

This child, she felt, needed her so badly. Hopefully her mother would return.

Joshua stood in the doorway when he glanced back at her. "Thank you for staying and taking care of her. She needs you. I needed your help."

After he walked out, her heart swelled with love as she glanced down at the sleeping child. Her own baby would have been six months old, and every time she thought of her, tears welled in her eyes.

Damn the baby's father. And now this child had been left in a terrible situation. Wiping her tears, she removed her clothes and crawled into bed.

But sleep didn't come easy as she thought of the man just up the hall. A handsome womanizer. A man that even if she felt attracted to him, and she did, she could never get involved with.

Men like him broke women's hearts and hers was just recovering. Life had dealt her three terrible blows all at once and the thought of being vulnerable again frightened her.

No, she would be returning to Fort Worth tomorrow.

CHAPTER 5

The next morning when he awoke, Kayla was up, dressed, and feeding Mia.

"We're running low on baby formula," she said. "I've got about three more bottles."

He ran his hand through his hair. Where was Skylar? Again, he tried to call her with no response. She must have partied so hard, she was passed out somewhere or still sleeping with some guy.

"What if she doesn't come back," Kayla said, speaking the words he feared.

"I don't know. She promised to be back yesterday. Hopefully, she's just running late and she'll show up here today. Can you stay with Mia? I need to get to work."

They were moving the cattle and that was his part of the Burnett operation. Cattle.

Of course, if he told his aunt what was going on, she would excuse him, but he needed to get out into the cool, fresh Texas air and clear his head. His job was to make certain that their cattle herd was well taken care of. And he enjoyed his job.

"I'll stay, but if she's not back by this afternoon, we're going to have to do a formula run," Kayla said. "This will last me through the day and that's it."

The thought of Mia going hungry again made him tense. No, she would not go hungry a second time. He felt remorseful enough already. Even if he wasn't her father, the child deserved to be treated better.

"I'll get back early. I'll tell the front gate to let me know if Skylar arrives and I'll be here in a flash. She's got a lot of explaining to do. First off, I want to know why she never told me she was expecting. And then she has some other questions to answer."

Kayla held the baby up to her shoulder and Mia burped a healthy sound.

He glanced at the two of them and suddenly didn't want to leave. It wasn't that he didn't trust Kayla because she had been wonderful. But the thought of going off and leaving them alone left him feeling desolate, empty. The smell of baby powder reached his nose and he had the urge to pick Mia up and hug her.

Leaning over Kayla, he gazed at the baby and she gave him a little smile, kicked her legs, and waved her arms. His heart warmed, and while it felt so very good, he didn't want to feel any emotions for this child.

Quickly, he pushed the feelings down. Feelings would make you hurt, so he did his best not to recognize them or feel them for anyone.

Last night, he'd lain awake in bed, asking himself what he

would do if she was his. There was no way he would ever marry Skylar. But what about Mia?

Didn't every child deserve a good home?

If she was his flesh and blood, then he needed to become a good father. Then the memory of Marcy and Patty came over him and he thought about his wild and crazy life. He wanted it to continue and there was no room for a baby in his world.

Leaning down, he smiled at the child. "Be nice to Kayla today. I'm going to work."

He gazed at Kayla who was watching him. "If you need me, I wrote my cell phone number on a piece of paper and laid it on the kitchen table. Or pick up the phone and dial zero. Security will find me."

"All right. Have a good day," she said as he walked out of the house.

It felt weird to leave someone in his home with a child. What in the world would she do all day besides taking care of Mia?

When he reached the barn, his other cousins were there. They all grinned at him. The news was out, and he was sure the entire Burnett clan knew he was a father.

"You just had to beat out the rest of us and become a father first," Tucker said.

"What are you doing home? Don't you have some celebrity you need to protect?"

"You missed the Christmas special. Kendra put on a television show at the clubhouse last weekend. You were gone. Oh, and Eugenia was looking for you. You're next," he said, smiling.

Last weekend he'd spent in bed with Marcy at her house. What a wild time. One he'd never forget.

Dear God, he'd forgotten all about the supposed ghost of his great-great-great-great-grandmother. The matchmaking ghost. And he'd left Kayla there in the house alone with the baby. What if she showed up?

"I'm not getting married," Joshua said as he lifted the saddle off the wall. Walking over to his horse, he began to cinch the saddle.

"That's what I said as well," Travis replied. "So when are you going to introduce your daughter to the rest of the family?"

Already he expected a phone call from his aunt Rose. The woman could be a tyrant and he didn't like the idea of explaining to her what was going on in his home.

"When are you going to contact your lawyer and see about a DNA test," Tanner asked.

His brother Jacob shook his head. Born two years after him, he was probably the most normal of the three of them. Smart and not a player like Joshua.

"I told you that sooner or later some woman was going to hog-tie you. Looks like Skylar is the winner," Jacob said, his deep sapphire eyes that reminded Joshua of Mia gazed at him with disapproval.

No, he would never marry Skylar even if Mia was his child. The woman was a spoiled, rich woman-child and he feared she would never settle down. Skylar reminded him of his mother and that was not what he wanted.

"I'm not going to marry Skylar. I don't even know if Mia is my child. Right now, I'm just trying to get through the day without my family giving me shit."

"Not happening," his young brother Justin said. "You said you would never get a woman pregnant and yet you did."

And he had never planned on it. He used protection every time he had sex. It's just that maybe the condom he used didn't protect as much as he wanted.

"That's not for certain," Joshua replied. "You can't believe everything Skylar tells you. I learned that real quick. I could be babysitting some other man's child."

Why that didn't feel right, he didn't know. But just one look at Mia's eyes and he thought she was a Burnett. And, damn, how had that happened?

"Gotta go," Tanner said. "There is work to do."

The dude ranch closed in November and they took the winter to remodel and update the cabins. But Joshua still had cattle he tended, and today, he needed that time away from people. Just him and several hundred cows.

Tucker grinned at him. "I'm going to spend time with my wife. Don't work too hard."

Justin and Jacob were whispering over in the corner. That couldn't be good.

"What are you guys talking about?"

"We were wondering if we should throw you a welcome-to-fatherhood shower?"

Did they not realize how much stress he was under? That was not funny in the least.

"It's not certain that I'm the father," he said. "No showers. Nothing. Now let's get to work."

Just then the security gate buzzed his phone.

"Is it Skylar?"

She had lots of explaining to do.

"No," the guard said. "Two Dallas policemen are here and they want to speak to you."

A trickle of fear spiraled through him. What in the hell did the police want to speak to him about?

"Tell them I'll meet them at the house," he said.

Why were the police here?

A feeling of foreboding overcame him and he turned to his brothers. "Work the cattle. I don't know if I'll be out there today or not," he said.

They both glanced at him, their sapphire eyes wide. "What's wrong?"

"The Dallas police are here and they want to talk to me."

Turning, he hurried toward the house, fear causing him to walk faster. What could this mean? He had a feeling it wasn't good.

CHAPTER 6

*M*id-morning, Kayla had just put the baby down to sleep. Bored, she wandered the house and then decided to see what was in the fridge for supper. She might not be here, but at least it would give her something to do.

She hadn't brought her laptop, so she couldn't work on her new business plan.

The house was straightened. She'd even washed Mia's dirty clothes. The baby was running out of everything, and if her mother didn't return soon, they would have to go shopping.

How could a mother go off and leave her baby like this? It was wrong.

Just then she heard voices outside. She glanced out the window and saw a Dallas police car. A trickle of unease wound down her spine and left her nervous.

What was going on?

Joshua walked up and led the uniformed patrol officers into the house.

Standing at the entrance between the living area and the kitchen, she smiled at the policemen.

"Good morning, gentlemen," she said. "Would you like coffee?"

"Ma'am," they said.

"Oh, no," the older man said. "Thank you."

"Have a seat," Joshua said and she could see he was nervous.

The two men sat on the couch, their expressions grim. "Nice ranch you have here," the younger officer said.

"Thank you," Joshua said. "Been in the family for generations."

"That's nice," the officer replied.

With a sigh, Kayla could see they didn't have good news. They were prolonging the inevitable.

"Do you know a Skylar Beal?"

"Yes, I've been trying to reach her," Joshua said. "What's wrong?"

The two men glanced at him. "What's your relationship to her?"

"We dated for about six weeks over a year ago," he told them. "On Friday, she dropped off her daughter at my house and told me I was the father. She was going to Dallas to shop and go to a party. Until then, I didn't know I had a daughter."

Again the two men glanced at one another.

"Her parents are Claire and Kenneth Beal," he said.

With a sigh, the one cop shook his head. "They're on a

cruise in the Mediterranean. They said they would get back as soon as possible."

"What's happened?" Joshua asked.

Kayla knew something terrible had happened for the Dallas police to reach out to him. They must be looking to make certain the baby was all right, because otherwise, why would they contact Joshua?

"Skylar was killed in a car accident early Sunday morning. Apparently, she'd been drinking and lost control of the Corvette. It flipped three times killing her on impact."

Unable to stop herself, Kayla gasped.

Joshua looked stunned, his mouth opened, his eyes wide and she could see he was in shock. He ran his hand over his face. "Dear God."

"The reason we're contacting you is because there were so many messages on her phone from you. We thought you might know what happened to her daughter. Her parents were very concerned about the baby being in the car with her."

Joshua sank down into a chair. "Like I said, she dropped the baby off at my house and told me I was the father. Kayla is here helping me take care of her."

The policeman nodded. "If you're the father, you have custody of her."

The other man glanced at him. "I'd suggest you get a DNA test to prove you're her father. I don't know if the grandparents will want custody of their grandchild, but her mother is not coming back to pick her up."

The older cop stared at him. "Do you want us to take the baby to child protective services?"

Anger spiraled through Kayla as she held her breath, fearing what Joshua would do. A baby put a cramp in his playboy ways. Until Friday, he didn't even know he had a child. Would he turn his own daughter over to the foster care system?

"No, I'll keep her until her grandparents return. Then we can make a decision about her at that time," he said before he turned to Kayla.

"That is if you'll stay and help me with her," he said.

"Of course," she agreed. This would be so much better than foster care. Poor little motherless baby. She would never know her real mother and that made Kayla sad.

There was no way she was going to leave this poor child now. Her next nanny job had just been secured.

The cops rose. "Sorry to deliver such horrible news, but we thought you needed to know. And we had to confirm that you had the baby."

"Thank you," Joshua said. "I've been wondering why she'd not returned. I tried to call her. Now I know."

Just then Mia started to cry. Kayla picked her up and took her into the living room.

The cops gazed at her. "How old is she?"

"We think three months old," Joshua told them. "I don't have her birth certificate, nothing to prove she's mine."

"Contact a lawyer," the cop said. "I think you're going to need one." They opened the door and walked out.

Kayla gazed at Mia then handed the child to Joshua.

"What are you doing?" he asked surprised.

There was so much to do now that Mia would be staying at the ranch for a while. She would be as well.

"I'm going to make a list of what we need. We've got to go to the store."

"I've got to contact my attorney," he said.

"You've got to change your daughter's diaper first," Kayla said.

This was his life for now. At least until her grandparents returned from their cruise.

For a moment, she thought he was going to argue with her, but then he took Mia into the spare bedroom and she heard him talking to her while he changed her diaper.

"I'm sorry, Mia. Your mom was a good woman, but she liked to party way too much. I don't know what's going to happen now, but we'll figure it out," he told the baby.

Kayla smiled. At least he wasn't sending her away. Hopefully this was a sign that he was willing to keep her and be a father to her.

When he walked in carrying her, Kayla smiled. The baby's diaper was on crooked, but it was better than that first day when it had almost been to her knees.

"I need to go to my apartment and get my things," she said.

"Is there a baby store near where you live?"

"Yes." She had visited it several times when she learned she was expecting. She'd even bought several outfits that she still had, though it broke her heart every time she looked at them.

The dreams of her own child wearing them was just too much.

Joshua held his daughter. "I'm her father for now. What am I going to do? I don't know how to care for a baby. I'm in way over my head. I should have given her to the police. What was I thinking?"

Kayla walked over to the handsome, terrified man and laid her hand on his arm. A sparkle of desire fired through her.

"Breathe. Skylar obviously trusted you enough to leave Mia with you. You said her parents were on a cruise in the Mediterranean and they let a nanny raise Skylar. Is that what you want for your daughter?"

Gazing at her, Joshua shook his head. "No, but what if she's not mine? Before I make my final decision, I need to learn the truth."

"Agreed," she said.

Removing her hand, Kayla walked away. What did it matter if he wasn't her father? This child needed a family. And the Burnetts obviously were one of the wealthiest families in the area. This would be the perfect location to raise a child.

Picking up her purse, she glanced at him.

"We don't have a car seat," she said. "We can't take her with us."

"What if I just give you my credit card and you go purchase the things we need for her?"

No, that would not be including him, and if Mia was his child, he needed to learn to participate in her care. Time to become her father.

"Mia is your responsibility. I'll go with you to get everything, but you really should have a part in this besides handing over a credit card."

"Call Samantha or Emily," he said. "Their number is on the phone list in the kitchen. See if one of them will keep her while we get supplies."

Knowing that Emily worked in the kitchen, Kayla tried Samantha first.

"Hi, it's Kayla, the nanny helping Joshua. We've had some bad news. Mia's mother was killed in a car accident. We've got to go to the store and pick up supplies. We don't have a car seat. Could you watch her? She's been so good since she's been fed."

"Oh my God, of course, I'll watch her. Bring her over to me. How is Joshua?"

"I think he's in shock," Kayla said. "The police just left. They were searching for Mia."

There was a moment of silence before Samantha said, "He didn't send the baby with them?"

"No, I'm going to stay on as his nanny until I'm no longer needed," she said. "Skylar's parents are due back soon."

Samantha squealed. "I'm so excited. And poor Mia. That poor child, I just feel so bad for her. Joshua is going to be just fine with you there by his side."

When she hung up, Joshua shook his head. "Let's get out of here before the family circles the wagons around us. Everyone will be coming by. How can a person's life change so drastically in just three days? How can it change so drastically with one police car?"

As much as she wanted to respond, she couldn't. Her own life had a drastic change like that. She'd gone from top salesperson, soon-to-be engaged, expectant mother, to nothing.

She'd been knocked to her knees by life just like Joshua was experiencing.

"We can't be gone long," she said. "She's running low on diapers and formula. And our little missy doesn't like going hungry."

"No, and she likes her formula warmed before she takes it,"

he said. Suddenly his eyes widened. "Oh my, what about her medical records? Her shots, when does she needs to see the pediatrician again? Where am I going to get that information? What kind of formula do we buy?"

Once again, Kayla laid a comforting hand on him. "We'll figure it out. For now, we need to get to my apartment and the store before they close."

He glanced around the house and then at Mia and finally Kayla. "My life will never be the same, will it?"

She gave a little laugh. "Probably not."

CHAPTER 7

*J*oshua was still in shock that Skylar was dead and he was now responsible for a baby. Possibly his baby.

While driving, he received the call back he'd been waiting for from his lawyer.

"Joshua, how are you?"

"I need your help," he said, thinking how surprised the man would be. For the next five minutes, he recalled the story to the one who had helped him with his mother's estate situation.

"Damn," the man said, "that's terrible."

"Yes," Joshua said, still thinking it was unbelievable that Skylar was dead and that he possibly had a daughter.

"First thing we need to do is prove you're the father. I'll have my secretary set you up with a company that does DNA testing. We'll also need to get the baby's birth certificate and see if Miss Beal listed you as the father. Then we'll need to file for custody of the child."

Terror filled him. Did he want to be responsible for a baby?

"Before we file for custody, I need to speak to Skylar's parents," he said.

Kayla glanced at him and frowned.

"Claire and Kenneth Beal are Skylar's parents," he said.

"The Beals who are in oil?" his lawyer asked.

"Yes, they're the ones," he said.

There was a pause. One that seemed forbidding.

"They have the resources to put up a fight if they want their granddaughter. You need to file now to show that you want her," the lawyer recommended. "The father has custody over the grandparents."

Right now, Joshua was overwhelmed with the events of the day. The way his life had suddenly and dramatically changed. Mia's sweet face came into his mind and his heart clenched. What if she was his daughter? Could he let her go?

"I can't make that decision today. Too much has happened. Let's find out about the DNA test and then we'll decide whether to file for custody."

There was silence on the phone. "You cannot show you have any doubts about raising her, or you need to let her go now. These people have the money, the resources, and the ability to take care of her if they want her. So don't hesitate or you could lose her."

The man had never steered him in the wrong direction and he knew what he was saying was true, but right now, his world had been turned upside down. What once was just a long weekend with a crying baby, now appeared to be a life-time commitment.

And he wasn't certain he could do a lifetime.

"Look, I'm on my way to purchase everything we need for a nursery. I've hired a nanny. I expect a summons from Aunt Rose at any moment. That's about all I can handle for one day."

The lawyer chuckled. "Aunt Rose is still in charge?"

"She'll be running the ranch from her grave." The news of the police showing up in front of his house would soon reach her and he'd be called in to find out what was going on.

"I'll have my secretary contact you with regards to the DNA test. Be prepared to take the test as soon as you receive it. We should get the results back in about a week. If you want custody, we'll need to file right away."

"Thanks," he said and disconnected the call.

Kayla sat in the passenger's seat and she seemed tense. "Do you always talk on the phone while you're driving?"

He glanced at her and frowned. "It's hands-free."

"You're the only parent she has left. What if you're killed in an accident?"

With a sigh, he knew what she said was true, but he'd never really been afraid of dying. He didn't live life on the edge. His biggest vice was women and that would certainly be curtailed for a while.

At least until he learned if Mia was his.

"I'll be more careful. I won't talk and drive at least until I know if she's mine or not," he said.

If something happened to him or Skylar's parents who would take care of Mia? She needed another set of guardians because already life had treated her unfairly.

Kayla shook her head. "What does it matter if she's yours

or not? You are the only responsible person in her life right now. She could be Joe, the bartender's, kid, but right now, you're her guardian."

"I agree. I was just thinking she needed another set of guardians in case something happened to me or her grand-parents."

Even though he was trying to resist the idea, he feared he was her father. Those big sky-blue eyes were a Burnett trait. All his life, he said he didn't want children, and yet, staring at her and thinking she might be his, his heart kind of melted.

But it would be the end of his philandering lifestyle. Did he want to change his life for a child?

"We need to talk about my position," Kayla said. "If you hire me full time, you will need to contact the agency I work for."

"Oh," he said. "I just thought that you could work for me until I made the decision."

Right now felt like he was juggling ten balls in the air. Nothing could be decided until he knew for certain he was her father.

"All right," she said. "I expect six hundred dollars a week with Sundays off."

"Oh no," he said, shaking his head. "We've seen the kind of damage I did. I need you to work seven days a week."

"Even I need a break occasionally," she said. "I'll also expect you to take care of her two hours in the evenings, so I can get that break."

"You'll still be in the house?"

"Yes," she said.

"I'll pay you one thousand dollars a week if you'll work seven days."

Kayla turned and stared at him. "You're crazy."

He laughed. "No, I don't want to take a chance on doing something wrong."

"If you're her father, you're going to make mistakes. Did your parents make mistakes with you?"

A rush of anger like a tsunami filled his chest. She didn't want to know the mistakes his parents made. The way his mother treated her husband and children. Kayla was his temporary nanny. Nothing more.

"My parents made me never want children," he said, almost gritting his teeth. "And now I'm in charge of Mia. Take the money and work seven days a week."

The woman's big beautiful emerald eyes widened in disbelief. He'd shocked her and that's what he wanted to do. He wanted her to know why he couldn't be left alone with Mia. He'd already proven he didn't know how to take care of her.

"Only, if you let me have the two hours at night alone."

"You got a boyfriend you want to spend time with?"

She was a beautiful woman. A woman that if she wasn't taking care of Mia, he would be chasing after. Maybe there was someone in her life she loved.

"No boyfriend," she said. "The store is at the next exit."

Putting on his blinker, he slowed and exited the freeway. If she wanted him to be safe, he would show her just how safe he could be.

"Give me the two hours in the evening and we have a deal," she said.

"All right. But what am I supposed to do with her during

that time," he said, feeling incredibly frustrated that his life had been upended completely.

"Get to know your daughter. Play with her, love on her, talk to her," she said.

Shaking his head, he couldn't imagine what they would have in common. "All right. We'll watch football together."

Kayla laughed. "I'm sure she'll love it."

After they parked his truck, Kayla took out the list and they exited his vehicle.

"Grab a buggy. We're going to need one, possibly two," she said.

He glanced at the list. "A baby needs all this?"

She turned and smiled at him. "You have no idea."

Walking through the store, he felt so out of place. There were other men shopping with their pregnant wives or men who pushed a buggy with a child in it.

This would be his life if Mia was his daughter.

They went to the diaper aisle and she filled the basket with three packages. Then they went to the formula and she bought three cases. Next, they were at the clothes aisle and she bought six little diaper sets and several things she called *onesies*, along with one cute little Christmas dress.

"What's that for?"

"Christmas is only three weeks away," she said. "We'll need to get her a gift from Santa."

"The baby is not going to know about Santa," he said. "She's not old enough."

She glanced at him and smiled. "No, but it's never too early to let her experience the joy of Christmas."

Panic began to set in. Christmas and birthday parties and

holidays and school. Oh my God, eventually she would go to school. He wasn't cut out to be a parent. What was he doing?

Licking his lips, he began to breathe heavily.

Kayla turned and gazed at him. "Deep breaths. You're going to be okay."

"No, I'm not. I will never be a good parent. She deserves better."

A man standing in the aisle next to them started laughing.

"First-time parent?"

"Yes," he said, wondering why he had said his thoughts out loud where someone could hear him.

"Take a deep breath. You'll do fine. I thought I had killed our baby when I accidentally dropped him. I was devastated. But he was fine. Looked up at me and giggled while I was leaning over him panicking. He's ten now. You got this."

Joshua felt embarrassed. Everyone in this store were parents or soon-to-be parents and he'd just gotten the job because of an accident.

"Thanks," he said and pushed the cart farther down the aisle. What was he doing here?

Kayla walked up beside him, laughing.

"Don't say a word," he said, shaking his head. "I can't be the only man who has ever questioned whether or not he wanted children."

"No," she said. "A lot of men don't want children, but you should have done something drastic to keep from having a baby."

"No way," he said. "I'm not going to neuter myself."

She laughed. "It's not neutering. And you wouldn't find yourself in the position you're in now."

49

That was true. But he liked having sex. He liked that he had swimmers, only they weren't supposed to be Olympic athletes charging through a rubber.

"There is a lot of danger involved when a man gets 'fixed,'" he said.

Kayla laughed and threw in a baby bed carousel.

"What's that for?"

"To entertain her," she said. "Oh, and we'll need a swing."

"A swing? Isn't she a little young to be thinking of a swing set?"

Was the woman going to buy out the store? This seemed like she was going overboard.

"Not an outdoor swing. A baby swing," she said.

"Oh." Why was he even asking questions? He knew nothing.

"Look, at this," she said. "It's a game she plays while she's lying on the quilt."

"I think she's a little young for games," he said. "All she does is eat, burp, fart, and poop."

"True, but she's holding her head up and looking around. The bright colors will get her attention. Games like these will help her development."

The nanny put the game in the basket which by now was overflowing.

"I think we've got everything, but a bed. We need to go over and look at those."

He glanced at his watch. It was getting late. "We need to hurry."

"You got a hot date?"

"No, but I hate to impose on Samantha any longer than

necessary. Mia could be even now screaming, making her wish she was not pregnant."

Kayla walked toward the cribs. As she gazed at them, he thought he saw a tear well in her eyes, but he wasn't certain. Why would this very smart, intelligent woman become a nanny? It just didn't feel right.

"You pick out the one you want. All I ask is that we get a changing table and a rocker that goes with the set."

Why did she think he knew which one would be the best? "Just pick one. Why do we need a changing table and a rocker?"

"Babies like to be rocked to sleep. And a changing table is nice because you don't have to bend over and break your back changing them."

"Oh," he said. "Just get one."

Watching her decide, he liked the one she chose and that made him feel better. It was a wood-stained bed.

"Now we need a mattress and bumper set."

"Good grief? This child is costing a fortune." How was he going to get it all in his truck?

Turning, Kayla glanced at him. "Did we spend too much? If you can't afford all this, let me know."

"Just get it and let's get out of here. I feel like I'm on baby overload. It's been a hell of a day and I want to sit in front of my television, drink a beer, and foam at the mouth."

Nodding, she gave a little laugh. "We'll have to put a lot of this together."

With a groan, he realized she was right. His night would be spent setting up a nursery.

"All right, I think that's it. We'll need a baby highchair

when she's six months old, but for now, let's get a car seat and we're done."

Glancing at the two shopping carts filled with baby stuff, he shook his head. How did families who were less fortunate than he buy all this stuff?

When they got to the cashier, he handed her his credit card.

She smiled at him. "New baby in the house? How wonderful. Did you have a boy or a girl?"

It was all he could do to keep from saying *just ring it up*. "A girl. A very expensive little girl."

"Oh, how fun," the lady said.

A clerk had to bring the bed around and they loaded it into his truck. When Kayla climbed in, he glanced at her. "Where to now?"

"The Texas Weekly Hotel," she said. "They're just down the street."

"That's where you live?"

"Between jobs, yes. No sense in paying for an apartment if I have a job. I'm at twenty-four seven."

With a sigh, he turned the truck toward the cheap hotel. Maybe he should be paying her more.

When he pulled up in front of her unit, he glanced at her. "Do you need help?"

"No, just give me some time to pack. Most is already in suitcases, but I need to grab my computer and cosmetics."

He watched her go inside and fewer than thirty minutes later, she pulled out a large suitcase, a duffel bag, and a briefcase. How could this woman live with so little?

Jumping out of the truck, he lifted her suitcase and duffel bag and put them in the truck. She was moving in with him.

And that felt weird.

While she'd spent the last night there, it wasn't until this moment that the thought of her living beneath his roof really hit him. They would be sharing the same space.

It would be like living with someone without the fringe benefits. And he liked what he could see of the fringe benefits. It would be hard not to sample them.

She went to the office, turned her key in, and then came back.

With a sigh, she gazed at him and he had the most incredible urge to kiss her. Why, he didn't know, but her full cherry lips were beckoning him and he knew that was not possible.

"Let's go get the little terror," he said, gruffly wondering what else life had in store for him this week. But, damn, was he ever thankful Eugenia hadn't shown up.

CHAPTER 8

*W*hen they got back to the ranch, Joshua was shocked to see most of the family at Travis and Samantha's house. Even his Aunt Rose was there.

Which probably meant he was in trouble.

"Get ready," he told Kayla. "You're about to meet the entire family. Looks like they're getting to know Mia."

Travis answered the door and gazed at Joshua. "Samantha told us what happened. How are you doing?"

A range of emotions filled him and he knew her death had affected him.

"I'm scared shitless," he told his cousin. "You got to choose being a father. I'm a single man who's already screwed up taking care of her once. Now she's mine until her grandparents return."

A big grin spread across Travis's face. "She's beautiful. She's fine and we've had so much fun this afternoon practicing with her. You're going to do great."

Oh good grief, his family was using his daughter as their

guinea pig. She was the test baby. Three pregnant women sat in the room, passing the baby around. This child would be so spoiled by the time her cousins arrived. Her cousins?

He pushed the thought out of his mind.

Aunt Rose met him at the door, frowning. "You should have told me what was going on."

He'd known this was coming, but right now, he was so tired, he didn't know how much more he could take. His life had been tossed into a bingo blower and instead of letters, it kept spitting out some new change for him.

B1 — A baby.

N29 — A nanny.

G65 — Ex-girlfriend killed and you're the new parent.

"We were almost out of formula and diapers. Plus, we wanted to get some things for the baby like a crib. I didn't have time to speak to you, and I knew you'd be here waiting on me when I returned."

The old woman had the audacity to grin at him.

"We? Who is this young woman? I hope you didn't bring home one of your ladies," she said. "You must become a responsible young man now that you're a father."

Embarrassment flooded Joshua. "She's the nanny, Aunt Rose."

The old woman smiled like she'd enjoyed embarrassing him.

"Oh, nice to meet you. I'm Rose Burnett and I run the Burnett Ranch," she said, gripping Kayla's hand.

"Kayla Scott. I came to interview with Emily and Samantha then Josh needed my help."

His brothers and his cousins and their wives were all gathered in the living room. The pregnant women were taking turns holding Mia and she seemed to be delighted to be the center of attention.

Aunt Rose glanced into the room. "Look at them. What a delightful scene. The women holding the baby and the family gathered around celebrating her arrival. I'm so happy to see another generation of Burnetts. And your child was the first of many more."

This was what he feared. His family getting attached to Mia. "We don't know for certain that she's my daughter."

The old woman let out a cackle that could have wakened the dead. "Are you kidding me? Did you see those eyes? She's got the Burnett eyes."

His brothers glanced over at him and grinned. They were enjoying his discomfort and the fact he was on the hot seat with Aunt Rose. No one wanted to be on the wrong side of Aunt Rose.

"Well, we'll wait until the DNA results are in before we decide she's mine."

No matter what he said, he could see they had crowned Mia the next generation of Burnetts and they were celebrating her arrival.

Mia gave a little cry and Kayla immediately went toward her, but the women weren't ready to release her. This was what he liked about the nanny. She was precise with her job and she took good care of the baby. Or at least, she had so far. For him, she'd been a godsend.

"Everyone, meet Kayla. She's Mia's nanny."

His aunt's brows rose like she didn't believe him.

"Don't be surprised if you see your ghostly great-grandmother in your home. Once she learns about that baby, she'll be there to check out the next generation."

Joshua wasn't certain he believed in the matchmaking ghost, even though his cousins were all married supposedly because of her. But a ghost? Come on. Besides, his single life would remain unchanged. There was no marriage in his future.

"I'm not worried," he told his aunt.

"Kayla will be staying in the guest room of my home," he told his aunt who had watched her hurrying to the child.

His aunt shook her head and gave a long sigh. "And how long will that last? She's beautiful. You're a hound dog and women don't stand a chance against a man like you. Especially when Eugenia comes around."

"Eugenia?"

"Your great-great-great-great-grandmother. The matchmaking ghost."

Hell, he didn't even know her name. He'd heard there was a ghost on the property, but frankly, he thought the family had either imbibed too much alcohol or had overactive imaginations.

There was no ghost.

He glanced at his aunt. "Kayla is taking care of the baby and nothing else. And a ghost is not going to change that."

The old lady shook her head. "If you sleep with her, you're going to have to clean the hog pen."

No one liked to clean the hog pen. It was a thankless, nasty job and he often wondered why they even did it. The hogs didn't seem to care they were rolling around in their own poop.

Watching Kayla cross the room, he liked the sway of her hips, the way she gave him shit about the baby, and even the way she laughed at him in the store. But he wanted to prove to his aunt that she was wrong about him.

"And if I don't sleep with her, I get the use of the company plane one weekend."

She frowned. "You're on. But I will be checking on you."

Like he could stop her.

"Now, you all will have to excuse us," he said, raising his voice. "We have a truckload of baby furniture to put together."

The Burnett men all looked at him and grinned. "Do you need some help? We'll soon be putting our nurseries together and could use the experience."

There was so much, and the day had been excruciating long. "Yes, please. We have a baby bed, changing table, and a rocker."

The women all oohed and aahed.

"We want to see the nursery after you get everything set up," Samantha said.

"We should throw Joshua a baby shower," Emily cried.

His heart slammed into his chest. "Oh, hell no," he replied. "Don't grow too attached to Mia until we get the results of the DNA."

These women were baby vultures. They didn't want to let her go and they were hovering around her like they were ready to pounce.

"Let me know if you need anything," Kendra, the celebrity of the family, said.

His aunt just cackled with laughter. "Josh, you are a stubborn Burnett man who is fooling himself if you believe that child isn't yours. Now it's getting dark and I'm going to get into the golf cart and toddle on back home. If you need more time off or anything, let me know."

The old woman hugged his neck and whispered into his ear. "Mia's beautiful. Accept that she's yours. And that Kayla seems like a nice young woman. Don't screw things up with her. Keep it in your pants."

Exasperated, he accepted her hug. "I'm very capable of keeping it in my pants."

Only his swimmers couldn't seem to stay inside a rubber.

"Sure you are," she said, not sounding convinced at all. She released him and walked out of the house.

He had thought about Kayla, imagined her curves, and wondered how they would fit in his hands, but she was taking care of Mia, and he had to keep things on a strictly business level.

With a sigh of relief, he stepped farther into the living room. He glanced at the baby who was held by Emily. Her blue eyes glanced up at him and she kicked her little legs excited to see him.

"I think she recognizes you," Emily said.

"She knows I was the one who almost starved her to death," he said, the urge to pick her up strong within him, but he resisted. She blew him a raspberry. Why was she doing this to him? She was wrapping her little hands around his heart and squeezing. And his family was being charmed by the baby.

His brothers came to his side. "You know, I think she has mom's chin."

Oh dear God, she did not look like his mother. Never. And

even if she did, he would never admit it. Mia was her own self, no one else. She looked like her dead mother.

"No," he said.

"No, really," Jacob said. "Look at it. It's kind of pointed like Mom's was."

He glared at his brother but did not respond.

"I'm just sad that Dad isn't here to meet her. You know he would have loved to see a little girl in the family," Justin said.

Joshua wanted to groan. They had all unconditionally accepted Mia, so why couldn't he?

Thank goodness his phone rang and he glanced down at the number. "I've got to take this."

He walked outside, the cool Texas night air a welcome relief from the tension inside.

"Hello," he said, dreading this conversation, wishing he didn't have to speak to this man.

"Joshua," the voice said. "Kenneth Beal. The police told me they spoke to you and that you have our granddaughter."

"Yes, sir," he said.

"Is she doing all right?"

"She's fine," he told the man. "I've hired a nanny to help me take care of her."

"Good," the man said. "From a reputable agency?"

"Yes, she was here interviewing with my sister-in-law. I kind of stole her from my brother and his wife."

The cold December wind blew and Josh didn't know what to say to the man who'd lost his only daughter. What did you say to a man who he imagined was devastated?

"We're in the middle of the ocean and there is nothing we can do for Skylar or Mia, so we made the decision to continue our cruise. We'll be home two days after Christmas. Is that all right with you?"

By then he would know if she was his daughter or not and he could make the decision at that time.

"Have a good time, sir. I'm sorry about Skylar. Can you tell me why she never told me she was pregnant?"

The man sighed. "We tried to get her to contact you, but as you know, she always did things her way. She wanted to raise her daughter by herself. And now she's gone. She won't be here to watch Mia grow."

That was a sad thought, but he wondered why she didn't want to tell him. Of course, how would he have reacted to her news? Not good.

"Again, I'm sorry, sir," he said. "Try to enjoy your cruise."

"Good-bye, Joshua," the man said.

Joshua ran his hand through his hair. Glancing up at the stars, he thought about what Skylar had said about her parents. How could a parent continue a cruise when their daughter had just been killed? How could they have a good time?

He'd have been on the first flight home. Even if he had to book a private jet.

How could he give up his daughter to parents who weren't rushing home?

Shaking his head, he sank down on the steps not wanting to go back inside or hear the laughter whenever Mia cooed.

"What am I going to do?" he said out loud.

Kayla appeared and sat on the steps beside him. A musky scent that was pleasant and the smell of baby wafted over him.

SYLVIA MCDANIEL

He liked the way she smelled. It reminded him of silky sheets and soft moonlight.

"You're going to take each day one at a time. You're going to wait until the DNA results are in and then you'll decide at the right time. But for tonight, it's time we took the baby home. I've got to bathe her and put her to bed if you can find me the infant bathtub we bought."

Reaching out, he grabbed her hand, thinking she was the only person who understood what he was going through. A pulse of electricity shot from her hand to his groin.

What the hell?

"I don't know what I would have done without you these last couple of days. Thank you. I'm so glad you're here."

She grinned at him. "Even when I tell you not to talk on the phone and drive?"

Shaking his head, he smiled. "Even then. Let's go rescue Mia from my family. It's time to take her home."

CHAPTER 9

*B*efore Mia, Kayla had only had one other job as a nanny. She'd enjoyed taking care of a rambunctious little boy until his parents moved to New Zealand.

But taking care of Mia, this sweet, little motherless child was a dream come true. They had spent two days setting up the nursery and now Mia had her own space. Kayla was doing her best to get Mia on a routine. One that would help the child settle in. One that would help Joshua have time with the baby.

She had yet to open her computer and continue working on her business, but hopefully tonight that would happen. It was time to put her thoughts on paper and do the necessary work.

Dinner was almost ready. Joshua told her she didn't have to cook, but she enjoyed making dinner for the two of them. All her life, she hated eating alone and did her best to have dinner with a friend or out somewhere.

Here, she was cooking and enjoying eating with Joshua

and even Mia. The little girl was swinging in the baby swing watching her set the table. Every so often she would blow a raspberry and coo. It was the sweetest sound, and Kayla would turn and smile at her.

After dinner would be bath time, and tonight, she was going to let Joshua bathe her. If he was going to be her father, he needed to learn how to take care of her.

She heard him walk in through the back door.

"Wash up, dinner is ready," she called.

He strolled in looking beat. The first place he went was to Mia, who kicked her legs and waved her hands at him. A little grin spread across her face, her large blue eyes dancing with happiness.

"Hello, princess," he said. "Were you good today?"

She was so excited and Kayla couldn't help but smile. How could the man not be moved by this child?

"Do I have time for a shower?" he asked.

"Hurry," she told him.

The thought of all those muscles being scrubbed beneath the hot water spray had her chest pounding. The way he would come out smelling fresh and clean and so delicious had her taking a deep breath, telling her body to back down. He was her employer, nothing else.

The man was a gorgeous hunk of male and his blue eyes and dark lashes could have a woman swooning. Women were an easy target for his good looks.

And she knew without a doubt that he was a womanizer. Three women called this afternoon and asked where Joshua was and who she was. When she told them she was the nanny, most of them hung up on her. But not one.

That stubborn woman refused to believe her.

A few minutes later, he was back in the kitchen, his hair wet, smelling of soap with a light fragrance. Some kind of manly smell. She licked her lips not wanting to think about him being wet in the shower.

"This looks good," he said. "You're going to cause me to gain weight."

"I like to cook," she said. "Tonight, I thought you could give Mia her bath."

His eyes widened and he shook his head. "No, I'll drown her."

She grinned at him. Almost starving Mia had traumatized him more than the baby. "No, it's really easy with the baby bath."

A frown crossed his face. "I know after dinner is your time, but could you show me what you do when you bathe her? With your help, I'd feel better."

"Yes," she said. "But that means you will have to feed her and put her to bed tonight."

It would be good for him to spend time with the child. He'd watched her doing this the last few nights and he could handle preparing her for bed. The only way for him to become comfortable taking care of Mia was for him to be involved in the baby's life.

"All right," he said and she could see concern in his eyes.

"What's wrong?"

"The lawyer called today. We're to take her in tomorrow and do the DNA test," he said. "Can you go with me?"

"Of course," she said, thinking this was the beginning. Soon they would know the truth about Mia. Soon he would have to choose whether to keep her or let her grandparents have her. "Are you nervous?"

With a sigh, he nodded. "Yes and no. I'll be glad to know the truth, but then I'll have to make the decision."

She nodded. "Raising a child is a big responsibility."

"Yes," he agreed. "I just don't know if I'm cut out to be a father. I always swore I'd never have kids."

At the moment, she couldn't imagine someone not wanting children. Because of her life, maybe she was biased because she wanted a family of her own more than anything. So she couldn't understand why he would not want kids.

"Why do you feel that way?"

He gave a little laugh. "Let's just say that my family was not the best. Everyone looks at the Burnett ranch and thinks we're one lucky family, but sometimes we have a bad egg or two. I came from the side that had the rotten-to-the-core eggs."

She was tempted to tell him her situation. It hadn't been much better. It was one of the reasons she wanted a family. A chance to have what other people took for granted. A chance to give love and receive love.

"Look around you. There are some good people here. You and your brothers seemed to have turned out fine. Seems to me that the odds of a bad egg coming from you is slim."

"But why take the chance? Maybe it's just better to let my line die out, so that nothing bad can be repeated."

If that was the case, maybe she should never be a mother, after her own mother had deserted her.

Picking at the food on her plate, it was hard to argue with that logic. "Is this why you like women so much?"

He glanced up at her and stared at her with those sapphire Burnett eyes. The ones that left you feeling weak in the knees. The ones women found hard to resist.

"Yes," he said. "I learned from the best. No commitments. No promises of forever. We have a good time and then it's over. I always use protection. That's why I'm shocked that Skylar thought Mia is mine."

Did men not understand that sometimes birth control didn't work? Condoms broke. Birth control pills failed. And everything else, she felt was just a waste of time. Except maybe an IUD, but that she would never try.

"Sometimes birth control fails."

"Apparently," he said.

They ate in silence for several minutes, each lost in their own thoughts. All Kayla could think about was what if Mia wasn't Joshua's. What would the man do with the baby then? Would he keep her until her grandparents returned?

Hopefully, it wouldn't come to that.

"Oh, by the way, three women called you today. Beth, Georgina, and Vicki. Beth and Georgina hung up on me when I told them I was the nanny. But, Vicki, she gave me hell. Told me I was lying to her and when she saw you again, she was going to kick your ass for cheating on her."

With a sigh, he shook his head. "Vicki is an airline stewardess who I see once every three or four months. I haven't seen her since August. We both are seeing other people. Beth, she only calls me when her boyfriend and her have a fight. Georgina only calls when she can't get a date and she wants sex."

Kayla laughed. "They sound like real winners."

As he chewed his food, she could see him contemplating the women. "You're right. They aren't women I would bring around the family. They're just looking for a good time and I make certain they get what they want."

As he put his fork down, he stared at her. "What about you? You dating anyone?"

"Nope," she said. "I'm taking a break from men."

"That sounds boring," he said.

"No, it's not. Man whores are not my kind of men. Players, womanizers, I'm done with all of them. Not worth it. Maybe I'll date again later, but for now, I'm enjoying being alone."

A frown crossed his face and he shook his head. "Seems really dull."

"It's not. I've learned a lot about what I want since I gave up my last relationship. When you think you have it all, you often overlook things about the other person that you don't like. It's only later that you realize that was all wrong, and yet I thought it was great."

Standing, she started clearing the table. She wanted to help him bathe Mia and then it was time to focus on her business. On what she wanted and not on Joshua.

He helped her clean the table and with her hands full of dishes, he bumped into her at the kitchen sink. Heat spread through her and she had to ignore the temptation.

"Oh, sorry," he said.

Her eyes widened at the feel of his muscled legs and chest.

"Why don't you finish clearing the table and I'll load the dishwasher," he said.

That was a good idea. It would keep them separated and not touching one another. "All right," she said, thinking at least she would not be rubbing up against his hardened muscles.

Thirty minutes later, everything was in the dishwasher and the leftovers were in the refrigerator.

"Time to bathe, Mia," she said, pulling out the tub that fit in the kitchen sink. It was a piece of foam cut to the right proportions that Mia could lie back in.

"Make certain the water is the right temperature. You don't want it too hot or too cold or else she'll get chilled."

He lifted her out of the baby swing. Her bottom lip trembled and she gave a little whimper.

"She likes that swing," he said.

"I told you so," she said. "She doesn't like it when you take her out of it."

They laid her on the foam and removed her clothes. Then Kayla filled the sink with water. With Mia getting attention from both of them, she cooed and kicked her legs.

Kayla handed the washcloth to Joshua and the baby soap.

"She's ready," she said.

His large hands were almost a third of her size as he put some soap on the rag and began to rub her down.

She kicked her legs and splashed him with her hands, laughing.

"Hey, you," he said. "You're getting me wet."

A smile crossed her face.

"You think that's funny?"

He reached down and tickled her tummy. Her eyes widened and then she gave a sound that almost sounded like a laugh.

"Damn, she's adorable," Joshua said and glanced away.

The man might not want to admit it, but he was getting attached to the baby. They both were and it would be difficult to leave her.

Kayla took the spray nozzle, tested to make certain the water was the right temperature, and then sprayed the soap off her.

Her eyes widened and her mouth opened.

Joshua picked up the towel they had laid on the sink next to the baby.

"That's all we do?"

"That's it," she said. "The water temperature is the main concern. Oh, and keeping her hands away from changing the water to hot or cold."

He held out the towel and Kayla wrapped the babe inside. They carried her into the nursery and dried her off. She handed Joshua the pajamas and he put them on her with a fresh diaper.

"Now you can feed her and rock her to sleep," she told him. "She's ready for the night."

With a sigh, he shuffled to the rocking chair and sank down.

"I'll get you a bottle," she said, heading into the kitchen.

When she came back, he was staring down at the baby, cooing at her. Her big blue eyes were trying to say something and Kayla felt her heart melt. Joshua may not have realized it yet, but he was bonding with this child. It would be so hard to let her go.

"Here," she said.

He took the bottle and put it up to her lips. Greedily, the child sucked on the formula.

"What if she's mine," he said. "What will I do then?"

There was no way that Kayla was going to say anything to him.

"Only you can make that decision," she said. "Can you let her grandparents raise your daughter?"

That was the hardest question.

He gazed up at her, the baby in his arms sucking on the bottle. "This isn't going to be an easy choice, is it?"

"No," she said.

"I want what's best for her," he said.

"Welcome to parenthood," she told him.

Quietly she stepped out of the room letting them have time alone. But before she left, she gazed back in.

Joshua was staring at the child taking her last bottle of the evening. There was a look of love on his face and yet she also understood he had not decided anything yet.

But the man was coming around to the idea of being a father, and that she liked about him. Now if only he would recognize those feelings regarding Mia.

CHAPTER 10

*H*e was in so much trouble. Who knew baby girls could grab you by the heart and entwine the two of you together? Who knew that the Burnett's most promiscuous bachelor was suddenly falling for this child that may or may not be his?

And who knew that the nanny could look so hot?

Spending time at dinner and then cleaning the kitchen together, he was ready to make a move on Kayla. But that would get him in so much more trouble. Maybe it was just being here at home with the baby and not out chasing barflies that was getting to him.

The nanny was off-limits. Though his cock refused to acknowledge she was his employee. It wouldn't be proper. He'd made a bet with his aunt.

And he didn't like cleaning the hog pens.

He glanced down at the baby. If he made a move on Kayla, she would go running and then what would he do about Mia?

No, he promised he would keep his cock in his pants and he was going to.

And it appeared Kayla had been hurt by someone who must have been a womanizer. He'd like to know more information about what happened, but she didn't appear to want to tell him the details. After everything she'd done for Mia and him, he didn't want to cause her any more pain.

The smell of lavender filled the room and he wondered where the scent was coming from.

An old lady wearing a dress from the 1800s shimmered into view and gazed down at the baby in his arms. It was all he could do not to pull Mia as tightly as possible against him.

What the hell was she doing here?

"She's beautiful," the woman said. "Another generation of Burnetts. I'm so happy. Look at those gorgeous blue eyes. Definitely a Burnett."

As much as everyone said Mia was a Burnett, he still wasn't willing to believe. Gazing at the apparition, he wasn't afraid, but rather in shock.

"I'm your great-great-great-great-grandmother. I've been watching over you since you were a little boy. You may not have seen me, but I was there when your mother tried to hit you with the frying pan. It was because of me that she wasn't successful."

What did he say? The memory of that awful night still haunted him.

"I was there when she and your father decided to spank all you boys because you had gotten into cookies and eaten every one of them. Again, I held back the switch she was going to use on you."

Another memory that he really didn't want to think about. This must be the apparition that Aunt Rose mentioned that he didn't believe in.

"And when you hit your head and was knocked out while you were bull riding, I held your head in my lap and said soothing words in your ear."

After that, he'd given up bull riding and concentrated on surviving his home life. Being raised in a household where shouting was common was tough enough.

"Now you have a daughter," she said as the baby's eyes drifted closed. "She's a darling little girl, Joshua."

"If she's mine," he said softly, staring at the baby in his arms. If this was a ghost, would she know the answer to that question? "Can you tell me if she's mine?"

The ghost let out a light laugh. "Why do think I'd know that? I'm not an all-knowing being, dear. All I can tell you is that you've been given a wonderful gift. Don't mess it up."

And that was his biggest fear.

"I don't know what I'm doing. Kayla has been wonderful, and I'm glad she's staying until the Beals arrive. But I don't know what to do."

The ghost frowned. "Until the Beals arrive? And after that? Are you just going to revert back to your old ways? Give up Mia? Go back to those hussies you like to bring home."

"Hussies? Is that some pre-historic word for loose women?"

The ghost shook her head at him. "I should lock you in the bedroom with one of those girls," she said.

"Good, we'll have reason to stay in bed and have wild, carnal sex all night long."

The ghost gasped. "You're a naughty man."

"You're right, I am," he said. "I love every minute. But please tell me that you're not watching what goes on in my bedroom?"

Had the ghost seen him? Had she witnessed what went on in his room? No, she couldn't have, that would be disgusting to think of your grandmother watching. No.

The old woman laughed. "Hardly. I'd be too embarrassed. But how do you think those women would feel about me dropping in for a quick visit."

With a sigh, he shook his head. "Not good."

"You need to concentrate on that little one you have in your arms. Someone has got to take care of this child."

"If Mia is mine, I'll take that responsibility," he said, still not certain he wanted to become a full-time father.

The ghost smiled.

"Once you've bonded with a child, it's hard to let go. Can you really give her up?"

He glanced down at the child now sleeping in his arms. Warmth spread through him and the thought of letting her go suddenly pained him. Was she right?

"It looks to me that you and Mia are definitely connecting," the ghost told him.

Pressure filled him. If he kept Mia then he would need to hire Kayla full-time and he didn't think he could live with her without touching her. Both she and the baby were making him think and feel things he'd never thought would be possible.

"I'll have to give her up. I can't care for a baby, not full time. And Kayla is only mine temporarily. She'll be working for Samantha and Emily and maybe even Kendra when their babies are born."

He moved Mia up on his shoulder and burped her, then returned her to his arms where he continued to rock her. Now he understood why Kayla had insisted they needed a rocking chair. The motion put the child to sleep.

"There is a solution to your problems."

"What?" he asked.

"There's a woman in the next room who longs for a family of her own. You know she's good with Mia. I know you're attracted to her. Maybe you should consider courting her. Not bedding her like those other women you bring home, but courting her."

How did you court a woman? And did he want to court Kayla? Marry her and create a family together?

"That's not possible," he said in a rush, the thoughts going so against his nature. He'd never planned on marrying.

Since his parents' divorce, he'd made the determination to use women for sex and never get involved. It was safer that way. But was it?

"You know about the unhappy state of my parents' marriage. You know how things ended and yet you want me to marry Kayla and create more babies? No, it's never going to happen. I'm not the marrying kind, Grandmother. Why would I put children through what my parents did to us? That's cruel."

The woman sighed and shook her head. "You Burnett men are such a stubborn lot. You are not your mother or your father. You are your own individual. You will live life your way, and so far, I've not been impressed. Those hussies you bring home, especially that last one, they are just using you. You're a better man than that, Joshua. Prove to me that you can overcome your past and be a good, strong husband."

But that was the problem. From what he'd seen of marriage, he wanted nothing to do with it.

"Some Burnett men are not going to be as good as others. You can put me in the unmarried category because it will never happen."

The ghost put both of her hands on her hips. "We'll see about that."

Suddenly the apparition disappeared. Joshua ran his fingers through his hair and gazed down at Mia. She deserved a good father. Kayla deserved a good man. And Joshua was neither.

After rising from the rocker, he laid the baby in the crib and stood there staring at her. Tomorrow they would do the DNA test. Soon he would know the truth.

No matter what he learned, she was definitely a cute baby and he'd never realized how much they could wrap their hands around your heart.

CHAPTER 11

$\mathcal{K}$ayla had noticed Joshua was different this morning. He'd been quiet during breakfast, and after they left the clinic, he was grumpy. The baby had let the doctor swab her cheek and even tried to suck on the industrial-sized Q-tip.

Joshua on the other hand had complained the entire time about him trying to swab his tonsils. Very quickly, she learned that when he was nervous or uncomfortable about a situation, he complained.

The doctor had told them they should have the results within a week. Christmas was two weeks away, so that would give him plenty of time to decide the rest of his life.

"Are you hungry?" he asked. "We could stop in town and get a bite to eat."

"Sure," she said.

When they pulled up to the restaurant, he got out of the truck and came around to help her get Mia out of her car seat.

The baby was learning to make more sounds and when he lifted her, she made a little squeal of noise.

"You, princess, need to be quiet in the restaurant," he told her.

He carried her inside in her baby carrier.

Kayla walked beside them. Going into the restaurant, it looked like they were a family. The family she'd always dreamed of having some day. But that wasn't possible with Joshua. He was her employer. He was a womanizer, and yet her body didn't care that he used women for his gratification. But she did.

The waitress took them to a booth and seated them.

They put Mia on the bench and Kayla had to sit beside Joshua. His leg bumped hers and she could feel the rock-hard muscles beneath his jeans. Her mind wondered what his naked leg would look like and she almost moaned out loud.

In a matter of moments, the waitress took their order and then they sat there. What did they talk about? What did they have in common besides Mia?

After the waitress walked off, she looked up and David Frantz was walking toward her. It was a good thing she didn't have something she could pick up and throw at him.

The smarmy-looking handsome man who walked like he was about to bestow his divine presence onto her.

"Kayla," he said, gazing at her with a welcoming do-me smile on his face. "How are you?"

Of all people to run into, he was not the one she wanted to see. She moved a little closer to Joshua and laid her hand on his arm. She had to pretend.

"I'm good. How's the company?" she asked, trying not to show any emotion on her face.

"Dad's his usual self. We lost the Baker account and the Rylie account," he said. "I know they were your babies."

She had their information on her laptop. She would contact them to see if they would be interested in working with her.

"What a shame," she said. "They were so easy to please. I never had a problem with them."

It was a lie, but she'd never admit to it.

He glanced down at the child sleeping in the carrier. "I thought you lost the baby."

Damn him. He was a total idiot. Now Joshua would know that she had miscarried. He'd ask her questions and she didn't like to talk about the baby she could've had. It hurt too much. But this dickhead couldn't keep his mouth shut.

"Mia is not mine," she said.

"Oh," he said, looking at Joshua.

"David Frantz," he said, holding out his hand. "Kayla used to work for our company."

We also use to date, she wanted to say, but why admit she'd dated a womanizing idiot like David?

"Joshua Burnett," he said.

Kayla gave him her brightest smile, hoping to send him on his merry way.

"I'll tell everyone in the office I saw you. You should come back sometime and say hello," he said.

"Why?" she asked. "So your father can escort me out again?"

His face turned pink. "You know, I had nothing to do with that."

"Of course," she said her face contorted into a smile. "I'm sure the news of you dating an employee sent him into the stratosphere where only the rich and famous are welcomed. By the way, I heard you were engaged to some rich socialite. Congratulations. I wish you nothing."

Joshua had just taken a drink of his iced tea and choked.

"Good-bye, Kayla," David said and turned on his heel and hurried out of the restaurant.

She removed her hand from Joshua and slide over in the booth.

"Well, that was certainly interesting," he said. "I kind of feel used."

"Oh, get over it. Now you know how women feel."

A grin spread across his face. "I do believe you have a temper. Maybe even a mean streak. *I wish you nothing.*"

"What did you want me to tell him? Eat shit and die and take your pompous father with you? Actually, I should have said *I feel so sorry for your fiancée.*"

Joshua laughed. "You really hate him."

"Yes, I do," she said.

"Is he the one who made you decide to take a break from dating?"

Why this was any of his business, she didn't know. "Yes," she said. "I lost everything because of him."

"What marketing company is he with," he asked her.

What could it hurt to tell him? "Frantz Marketing Company," she said.

"Wow," he said. "They're a premier marketing firm."

"Yes," she said. "I made them lots of money until his father found out I was dating his son. A girl like me was not good enough for his boy. Who did I think I was?"

What had hurt the most was when he brought in the background report he'd had done on her. A girl raised in a foster family was never going to marry his son. Though she graduated college at the top of her class and made his business a lot of money, the single fact that she didn't know anything about her mother and father disqualified her.

Her fists were clenched. All of the old memories of how they had embarrassed her by walking her out of the office in front of everyone left her furious.

Joshua reached out and took her hand. He rubbed her fingers until they uncurled. Warmth spread through her and she sighed.

"Do you want me to kill him?"

Stunned, she glanced at him as a grin spread across his face. "I wouldn't do it," he said. "But I'm sure we could find someone on the internet."

"Are you crazy?" she asked staring at him, feeling uncertain.

Joshua roared with laughter. "I loved the expression on your face. You were afraid I was serious."

People were nuts, and nowadays, you couldn't say something like that in jest. "Shh...someone might hear you and think you're serious."

"How about you settle for me having him banned from Burnett Enterprises?"

Brows raised, she glanced at him. "You would do that?"

"If you want me to, I'll tell our office to never use their services," he said a grin on his face.

She studied him for a moment. Their ranch was so large that they used a marketing firm? That was good to hear.

"No," she said, thinking it would be better to wait until she had her company rolling to approach Joshua about switching to her.

"Would you rather I hire someone to beat him up?" he said, reaching over and pulling her close against him. The heat of his body warmed her. His smell was comforting and she understood why women liked him so much.

"Now, you're just saying crazy shit," she said.

"You're right, but it was good for me to see how much of an ass a man looks like when he's treated a woman wrong."

Oh, if he only knew the half of it. She hadn't mentioned the miscarriage, though the idiot asked about the baby. She'd never told him that she miscarried and he'd never asked about the child she'd been expecting. His actions confirmed her suspicions that he would have been a terrible father. And his father would have been a horrible grandfather.

As much as she hated losing that child, it was for the best. But her heart still ached at the thought of her baby.

Why hadn't Joshua asked her about the miscarriage?

"I'm shocked we haven't run into one of your previous paramours," she said, trying to turn the conversation in a new direction.

"Oh, I'm sure that one day we will," he said as he released her.

The waitress brought the food to the table and they began to eat just as Mia decided that she was missing out on food.

Her cries had patrons in the restaurant turning in their direction.

"Give her to me and I'll feed her," Kayla said.

"No," Joshua said. "You eat your food and I'll hold her. Then we can switch."

Surprised, she watched as he lifted her from the carrier and held her while he pulled out a bottle.

"Waitress, can you heat this bottle," he asked.

The woman smiled at him. "Of course," she said.

Mia was beginning to let everyone hear her high-pitched wails by the time the waitress returned.

Joshua tested the formula on his arm, just like she'd shown him, and then he held the baby and fed her.

The man was getting better and better at taking care of Mia. And her heart was becoming more and more attached to the child and even the man. With a start, she realized she'd better be on her guard. No way in hell would she ever fall for another womanizer. A man like Joshua could very easily break her heart.

CHAPTER 12

*T*wo days later, the test results were delivered by special delivery. He'd been out working the cattle when he received the call from the gatehouse that he had a special delivery letter.

Knowing immediately what it was, he hurried to the security booth. With trembling hands, he rushed back to the house.

When he walked inside, Kayla was holding Mia. The baby had been crying and he could see she was upset.

"Is she all right?"

"I think so," Kayla said. "She's been fussy all morning. Why are you home?"

He held up the envelope. "It's the test results."

"Wow, that was quick," she said, putting Mia in the swing and turning the dial.

Staring at the envelope, he was confused about what he wanted. What if she wasn't his? Then what did he do? What if she was his? Could he forget his single life and become her father?

And what about Kayla? What would this decision mean to her?

Ripping open the envelope, he pulled out the results and the letter that went with it.

"She's mine," he said. "Mia is my child."

Kayla came over and pulled him to her side, she patted his back. It wasn't a full-blown hug, but a half hug.

"Congratulations."

Was it?

His knees begin to shake and he sank down on the couch. What the hell? Skylar would have kept his daughter from him if she hadn't gotten a wild hair and decided to go to Dallas. The thought sent a rush of anger like a tiger growling through him.

"Damn it, Mia is mine."

Gazing at the child swinging happily, a sense of pride and wonder overcame him. Mia was his. She was his blood, his child, and a sense of responsibility overwhelmed him.

Nausea overcame him. What had he done?

Kayla grabbed Mia's bag and removed her from the swing. She bundled her in the little jacket they had bought for her.

"Where are you going?"

"Just across the way. Samantha wants me to bring her over to see their Christmas decorations. I'm going to help her finish decorating. We're invited to dinner if you feel like it," she said.

"Sure," he said. "Give me a little time and I'll come over."

She reached out and touched his arm. A sizzle of awareness spiraled up through all the other emotions that had him in their grip. But this one he enjoyed. Glancing up at her, he didn't know what he would have done without her these last few days.

"I won't say anything. You're the one who should tell your family."

"Thank you," he said, leaning his head into his hands. That letter was good news and bad news.

"Do you want me to stay?"

"No, you go on." He needed time alone to process what he'd just learned. Everyone had been telling him, but he'd been too stubborn to believe that Skylar would keep this information from him. That he had a daughter.

And part of him was ecstatic she was his, but the other part of him, the single man, didn't want to give up his life. And babies didn't fit into a bachelor's lifestyle.

Kayla walked out the door with Mia, and it felt like his world came crashing in. Now he had to make the painful decision. Did he keep Mia or did he give her to the Beals? Those cruise-loving people who would probably put her with a full-time nanny.

She'd be raised by strangers while they saw the world.

But wasn't that what he was doing?

No, he spent time with her in the evenings. They had the ritual down now and he put her to bed, rocking her until she fell asleep.

The smell of lavender filled the air. No...

"Not now, Eugenia," he said. "Please, not now. I need some time to think without being interrupted."

The ghost didn't say a word at first, but just hovered there, watching him.

"Again, this is so simple. Marry Kayla. She can take care of Mia and give you many more children."

"What part of *I'm not getting married* didn't you understand?" he asked, his voice rising with frustration. The woman refused to leave.

"You're just fooling yourself. Just like you did with Mia's parentage. She's yours."

"You're right," he said, wondering how he could get a ghost out of his house. Samantha might know. She'd worked on a ghost-hunting show.

"Those gorgeous Burnett eyes showed her heritage and that precocious little girl is going to attract so many men when she's older. Even hound dogs like you," Eugenia said with a laugh.

His head jerked up and he glared at the ghost. "No. I'll shoot them if they show up here."

Now wasn't that an odd feeling? He thought nothing of chasing and winning a woman, but somewhere they all had fathers.

"But you're not going to have her. She'll be raised by her grandparents and turn out like her mother."

"No," he said, thinking he would never let her turn out like her mother. "She's a Burnett."

The ghost grinned. "Yes, she is."

Damn it, she'd almost convinced him that Mia needed to stay here, but he was so confused. He had to look at this from the angle of what was best for Mia.

"You're driving me crazy. I've got to get out of here."

The ghost laughed. "You're coming around Joshua. Let's just hope you see how good a woman Kayla is before it's too late. You need her."

Shaking his head, he glared at the ghost. The ghost needed to know.

"I do see how good she is, but like you said, I'm a hound dog and she doesn't need to get hurt again. She's had to deal with a man like me before."

"Then change and show her the kind of man you can become. A good man. A good father, and most of all, a good husband."

He'd reached his limit. Jumping up, he picked up his coat and hat and walked out the door. Just to make himself feel better, he slammed it behind him as he hurried to his cousin's home. It was sad that he had to get out of his own house. But Eugenia was driving him crazy.

The smell of lavender followed him.

"No," he said. "You can't go to Samantha and Travis's. Just no."

It would not be good for him to go into their house, screaming at an apparition. Someone might think the stress had finally gotten to him and call the van from the local mental hospital.

"Dear, I'm a ghost. I can do whatever I want to do. Including follow you. I just want to make certain that everything is ready for Christmas."

"Leave me alone tonight, Eugenia. I've got some heavy decisions to make."

"Yes, grandson. But you need to especially notice how beautiful Kayla looks tonight. In my day, we would say she looks quite fetching."

Shaking his head, he walked up the steps.

"All right, I'll be sure to look at her. Now, go away," he said, thinking he would try to avoid glancing at the woman at all costs.

Kayla opened the door. "Are you all right? Who were you talking to?"

"You don't want to know," he said and ushered her back inside and shut the door behind him.

Ghosts didn't need doors, but it made him feel good to shut it on Eugenia.

His cousins and their wives were all gathered around decorating the house for Christmas.

Travis grinned at him. "We're not letting the pregnant women climb on ladders, so we're here helping. Next, we'll do Emily and Tanner's house and then Tucker and Kendra's."

"I got the results of the DNA test back."

They all stopped what they were doing and gazed at him, their eyes wide. He could see the fear in them.

"And?" Travis asked.

"She's mine," he said. "She's a Burnett."

Everyone screamed and danced, and he wondered if he could ever let her go and keep his family's approval. Probably not.

Turning, he saw Kayla staring at him. A smile graced her face. Damn, but his grandmotherly ghost was right. She did indeed look fetching in her tight jeans and Christmas sweater. Long black boots clung to her legs and the way her blonde hair was curled around her face made him see how beautiful she was.

He walked toward her and his family all giggled. When he reached her side, he smiled at her.

"You going to be okay?"

"Yes," he said.

"Kiss her," Samantha cried.

"Kiss her," Emily said and pointed up to the ceiling above him where a mistletoe sprig was hung.

"It's tradition," Travis said, laughing. "You have to."

His family was all staring at them; he didn't know what to do.

"Do it," Tanner cried, smiling at him like they all knew that once he touched her, he'd be a goner and that was his biggest fear.

What was he supposed to do? He glanced down at Kayla staring up at him, and he could see the uneasiness in her eyes.

Finally, he decided it would be easier to kiss her than to try to explain to his family why he couldn't. That she was his employee. And besides, those full cherry lips of hers had been tempting him.

Days of watching the way she moved about his home, her full hips swaying when she walked, and those breasts. Oh, how he wanted to lean down, lift her shirt, and taste her sweet nipples.

Pulling her to him, he layered his lips over hers and was immediately swept away as desire rushed through him. What had meant to be a simple kiss became one he didn't want to stop. The taste of her was sweet and the feel of her body against his was enticing.

Kayla pulled back and gazed at him astonished. "I think it's time to take Mia home and put her in bed."

Right now, all he wanted to do was carry her home and put her in *his* bed.

But she was off-limits. She was his nanny. And he'd just broken a very important rule. Don't kiss the help.

CHAPTER 13

*L*ater that evening, Kayla was in the nursery putting the baby to bed. Mia was tired, her eyelids wanting to close, while she put her sleeper on her.

"You had a busy day, sweet girl," Kayla said.

She sat in the rocker and swayed with the baby while feeding the infant the nighttime bottle. Since she'd arrived, Mia had slept through the late hours and into the morning almost every night.

They had purchased a baby monitor and she kept the speakers in her room so she could hear Mia at night.

The baby's tiny hands reached up and she tried to clasp the bottle, but her fingers were too small. Already Kayla could see changes in her and she'd only been here two weeks. Christmas was a week away and she wondered how the Burnett family celebrated.

Would she be included or would she be on her own that day? Foster families included her when she was small, giving her a little something, while they would heap presents on their own children. It was always a letdown and she was glad when she went to college. She had the dorm to herself most big holidays.

Being alone was something she had grown accustomed to. It wasn't that she liked it, but what choice did she have? It would have been wonderful to live a normal life with real parents and cousins and grandparents.

And what she remembered about her mother was very little. It was like the first twelve years of her life happened to a different person.

Life had not given her the option of a family. Even in foster care, she kept hoping to find someone who would adopt her, but at the age of twelve, no one wanted her. So she stayed in foster care until her eighteenth birthday.

The family she was living with at the time told her she could stay through the summer until she left for college. But they'd never invited her back. Those were the families that hurt the most. They acted like they cared for you, but when you left, they never contacted you again.

Glancing down at Mia, she envied the baby.

"You're so lucky," she said. "You've been born into a wonderful family. I'm so glad you're Joshua's child. And soon you will have cousins."

Babies were adopted fairly quickly out of the system, but now Kayla would not have to worry that Mia would be in the childcare system. Right here on the Burnett Ranch, she would have her father and so many people who loved her.

The smell of lavender filled the room and she glanced around, wondering if there was a room deodorizer she didn't know about.

A vision appeared before her and it was all she could do not to jump up and run out of the room with the baby. For a moment, she thought she was seeing things.

An old woman dressed in clothes like in the 1800s stood before her.

"Hello, dear, don't be frightened. I won't hurt you or the baby. That child is my great-great-great-great-great-grand-child and I just had to see her. Oh, how I wish I could hold her. She looks so sweet."

Kayla stopped rocking and stared at the apparition. She'd never seen a ghost and she wondered why she was here now.

"Didn't the family tell you about me?"

"No," she managed to sputter out.

The woman laughed. "I'm called the matchmaking ghost because I like to make certain the family line continues. Ask Samantha, Emily, and Kendra about me. They've met me and I can't wait to see their babies. You may call me Eugenia."

Kayla pulled Mia a little closer. She would do whatever necessary to protect her.

"If you go to the main office, there are pictures of me and my husband and our three boys. The reason I got into match-making was because my stubborn sons refused to get married and give me grandbabies." She grinned. "But I found them three beautiful women who fit them perfectly. And I could do the same for you."

Oh, no. She wanted nothing to do with a ghost interfering in her love life. She didn't have one and that was probably for the best.

"Thank you, but no. Does Joshua know about you being here in the house?"

"Oh yes," she said. "Who do you think he was talking to this evening on the porch of Travis's house? Me. He was upset because I told him I thought you and him should marry."

Kayla gasped. "What?"

The man was handsome as sin wrapped in jeans and a cowboy shirt that clung to his muscular chest. And he was exactly the type of man she planned on avoiding. Yet tonight he'd kissed her under the mistletoe and that kiss had sizzled all the way down her spine, lingering in her center.

The man was her employer. She'd already been burned badly by falling in love with the boss's son. It wouldn't be good to go after the man who paid her weekly.

"A woman like you could settle Joshua down," the ghost said. "He's had some bad experiences in his past with his family. His mother was not someone I would have chosen for his father. But they ignored my suggestions and look how that turned out."

That reminded her of how Mr. Frantz had not wanted her for his son. She bristled and realized she couldn't do the same thing again. It would not be good to get involved with Joshua. It would be like getting involved with the boss all over again.

Shaking her head, she replied, "He's a womanizer. I don't date men who take advantage of women. I don't want a man who uses women like he does."

That statement was true now, but in the past, she'd dated some real losers.

Joshua had hinted at problems in his family, but she didn't know what had happened.

The ghost leaned over and gazed at Mia. "Such a sweet, precious child," she said. "You love children. You're getting attached to Mia. And I've seen the way you look at my grand-son. Don't deny there is no attraction there."

Oh, there was definitely an attraction. The kiss tonight had proven that. How long had the woman been around watching them? A shiver went through her.

"Do you want your own family?"

Of course, she did.

Kayla didn't respond but sighed and gazed at Mia. Her little girl would have been walking and babbling. Her baby had not survived. The anniversary of the miscarriage was next week and she didn't know how she was going to get through the day.

"Yes," she said, her chest aching, her heart breaking at the thought of her child.

"Where are your people?" Eugenia asked. "Do they live here in Texas?"

Why did people, even ghosts, assume that everyone had family? Sure, most people did, but there were some trapped in the foster care system who didn't know where to find their parents, they had been taken from them, or were left behind.

It was one of the reasons she wanted her own family so badly.

"I don't know. When I was twelve, my mother went to the store one day and never returned. The neighbors finally called Child Protective Services," she said, remembering that awful day. Begging them not to take her, that her mother would be back any moment.

"You need us and the Burnetts need you," the ghost said, clapping her hands together.

How did a family as wealthy and powerful as the Burnetts

need Kayla? She was just being nice. Sadly, no one needed her except Mia.

"You can help heal Joshua and he can give you the family you've always wanted," she said. "Your children would be perfect for Mia."

Thinking about the child that lived alone in the house for a week, eating out of cans and watching television until the wee hours of the morning, always drained her.

That child had no idea how her life was about to change when that car from CPS pulled into her driveway.

Standing, she was tired, the baby was asleep, and she had to stop thinking about her past life. Her focus needed to be on how she was going to create a company that would make her independent. Maybe she would continue to be a nanny, but if she got fired again, she would have something to fall back on.

Glancing down at Mia, she kissed her on the forehead. "Goodnight, little one. Sweet dreams."

She laid her on her back and the baby continued to sleep.

Turning toward the apparition, she sighed. "Joshua is his own man. He'll make his decisions on his own. As for me, I'm not interested in being one of his women."

The ghost shook her head. "That's a lie. You like him."

"Even so, he's not the kind of man I want to ever involve myself with again."

The ghost gave a little laugh like she didn't believe her. "You look tired. Let's talk about this again when you're ready."

So much had happened today. They found out the truth about Mia's parentage, the kiss with Josh, and now Eugenia. Confusion filled her. The ghost wanted them to marry, and while it would fill so many empty places in her heart, she wanted a man who loved her and wanted her, no one else. And she couldn't be certain that Joshua could settle down with one woman.

The ghost leaned over the crib.

"Go on to bed, get some rest. I'll watch over Mia for a while. Remember, things are always the hardest just when you're about to get your heart's desire."

Was this her heart's desire? Yes, she wanted a family, but she wasn't certain about Joshua.

A few minutes later, just as she was about to drift off to sleep, she heard Eugenia singing to Mia. The sound was soothing and yet she couldn't believe she'd seen a ghost.

CHAPTER 14

*J*oshua awoke to the sound of thunder shaking the house. The wind outside was blowing something horrible and lightning crackled in the sky outside. Just then the hum of the power went out, his bedside clock went black and he jumped out of bed.

Walking into the living room, he bumped into Kayla.

"Oh my God," she cried. "You scared me. I was looking for a flashlight."

"In the bottom kitchen drawer," he said, opening the door of the house and glancing outside. The wind was gusting and driving rain had him shutting it quickly.

"Do you think it's a tornado?"

"Don't know," he said. "Is Mia in the crib?"

"Yes," she said. "I checked on her and she was fine. But I thought I should find a flashlight in case we needed one."

Though it was dark, he could see she wore a long T-shirt type of gown.

Something hit the window of the house and he jumped.

"That's it. We're all in the closet," he said. "I'll get Mia."

"Which closet?" Kayla asked.

"The one in my bedroom," he replied. "It's in the center of the house."

When he picked Mia up, he saw that Eugenia was in the rocking chair. "Better go, ghost, I think we're having a tornado."

"I'm not afraid," she said. "What can it do to me? Lift my skirts?"

Joshua chuckled and would have stayed to talk to her, but he felt the need to get the baby in the closet.

Leaving the apparition in the baby's room, he walked to the makeshift tornado shelter. Kayla had brought a blanket from off the bed and she laid it on the floor for Mia.

The baby grunted but slept on when he laid her down.

Thunder boomed and the wind and rain slashed at the windows, but they were now as safe as they could be. Someday he intended to build a storm shelter. Maybe it was time to do that now.

"Have you ever had tornadoes out here before?"

They sat inside his closet on the carpeted floor. His clothes hung around them in the large room. It was here that he kept his guns in a gun safe. As they leaned against a wall in the dark, he couldn't remember a more intimate place to spend time with someone.

"A couple of years ago, we had a storm come through and take one of the neighbor's houses off its foundation. But that's about as close as I've come to one. What about you?"

She pulled her knees up and was leaning her head on

them. "One hit about two blocks from us. I've always been terrified of twisters."

"Me too," he said.

"It seems a little late in the season for one," she said.

Something large hit the house and she jumped.

Knowing they were both on edge with this storm, he pulled her up against him and wrapped his arm around her. "You're shaking."

"Yes," she said.

"So let's talk about fun things," he told her. "Where did you go to college?"

"I graduated from the University of Texas," she said. "I have a degree in marketing."

He knew this from talking to her when she first came to work for him, but hopefully it helped keep her mind off the weather.

"Did you love Skylar?"

"No," he said, glancing at the baby. "We were just each other's toy for a while. You know, I don't remember the condom breaking. I don't remember her getting upset or anything. Other women freak out when a condom breaks."

"Understandable," Kayla said.

"So tell me about this man you were dating," he said.

"Big mistake. You met him," she said. "His father didn't think I was good enough for his son. Frankly, I don't think his son is good enough for me."

That comment he loved.

Joshua laughed. "You have a strong spirit."

"Have to," she said. "Life has not treated me kindly."

"Were you pregnant with his child?"

"Oh, you caught onto that, did you? I was hoping you didn't realize that he thought Mia was his child. Bastard. When I lost the baby, I didn't call him and tell him, because by that time, I had been fired from the job I loved, and also, I'd been dumped by David. Why tell the man?"

A feeling of sorrow overwhelmed Josh. She had been through a lot.

She stretched out her legs and one brushed against his bare leg. He'd forgotten all about how little they were wearing. He was in his underwear.

Mia stirred on the blanket and then she went right back to sleep.

The wind slammed into the house and he worried that at any moment, the roof was going to come off.

"Did you know there is a ghost in this house?"

He laughed. "You met Eugenia."

"Yes, she tried to talk me into marrying you," she said, shaking her head.

"And she told me that the perfect woman for me was right in front of me," he said. "How did you respond?"

"I told her no," she said. "You're a womanizer."

"And I told her I never intend to marry," he said. "I bet she didn't like your answer."

Kayla laughed. "No, she didn't. Why are you so determined to never marry?"

Joshua really didn't want to tell her. In fact, he often thought he was crazy for acting the way he did, but he didn't know how to stop.

"My parents divorced when I was a teenager. For as long as I remembered, they were never happy. But mother went out of her way to embarrass dad. Her family was very wealthy and they were big social snobs. She would go to the country club and pick up a man. She and Pops would fight and then the next day, she would do it again. It broke my father's heart."

"And now you believe that all women are like your mother," she said.

"A lot of them," he replied, knowing how crazy that sounded.

"So you're getting even with all women for how your mother behaved. Or are you just acting like your mother?"

A shiver went through him. "No. I would never act like my mother."

"Sure seems like it," she said.

Could he be acting like his mother? No, he would never be like that woman.

"I agree my mother caused me to distrust women. I agree she made me never want to marry. So instead I tell a woman right up front that I'm not into relationships, marriage, or happily ever afters. She knows what she's getting into. Did David do that with you?"

She gave a little laugh. "No, but we tried to keep our romance out of the office. He told me it was not good for morale when one of the employees was dating the boss's son. Instead he was dating another socialite at the same time. The one he's marrying soon. Bless her heart, I hope she figures out he's not a good man before they say I do."

They sat in silence for a moment, listening to the wind howling outside.

"I should go check and see if the storm is passing."

"No," she said. "We can hear the wind still howling. Stay with me."

She laid her hand on his arm and he turned to her. Without thinking, his mouth slid over hers and he took possession, his lips controlling hers, while his hands slid up and threaded their way through her hair.

Oh, how he wanted her. If she were one of his women, he would be crawling on top of her and proving there was an attraction between them. There was this need to show her that he was a good man. He was a man that if not burned by life would've been like other men.

His hand slid down her chest and he felt the swell of her breast. Oh, how he wanted to push aside her T-shirt and place his mouth on her nipple.

A brilliant burst of lightning and a roar of thunder shook the house and Mia decided she didn't like thunderstorms. She let out a wail that could have awoken the house next door.

Kayla pushed him aside and picked up the baby.

"It's all right," she said, holding her, soothing the child.

With a sigh, Josh rose to his feet. He had to get out of this closet or lose his mind with wanting Kayla.

Stepping into the living room, he saw the flashes of light as the transformers blew and the tornado swirled in the distance.

Running back to the closet, he closed the door behind him. He pushed Kayla to the ground and they made room for the baby not to be squished.

"Tornado on the ground," he said as the house began to shake.

Kayla threw her arms around him and held onto him

while he held his daughter in his arms between them and prayed they would survive.

The house rocked and he feared that the roof was going to fly off, but in less than two minutes, the wind and rain subsided and they were out of the danger zone.

Mia had been quiet and he was shocked at how good she'd been.

Rising off Kayla, he glanced into her eyes. It was dark and so hard to see, but suddenly she pulled his head to her mouth and she kissed him.

He wrapped his arms around her and his mouth consumed hers like he would never let her go. Like she was the rock that held them together and kept them from blowing away.

The baby began to fuss and slowly she released him.

"I'm not ready to die just yet," she told him.

"Me either," he said. "I've got some unfinished business."

In the darkness, they walked out of the closet and were amazed the house was still standing. When he stepped outside, he saw part of the deck was gone, but that could be replaced.

Inside, he held a still-shaking Kayla. "We survived. But it's a heck of a mess outside. Downed power lines are everywhere. We're waiting until daylight to get out."

CHAPTER 15

As the sun came up, they could see the damage to the Burnett ranch. Even Eugenia shimmered in the window and glanced out at the downed trees and blown-off roofs of the guest cottages.

Thank goodness they were closed right now and no one had been staying there.

"Sometimes Texas weather is a real pain in the ass," the ghost said. "This is not the first time a Texas twister has caused damage and I'm sure it won't be the last time."

Kayla had a hard time talking to the woman. It just felt weird. Crazy. The woman had been dead for a long time, and yet here she was, and they were discussing the weather.

"Yes," she said. "Especially when cold and hot fronts mix. There is always trouble then."

There was no power. No heat. Nothing. The late winter storm had knocked out everything, and even now, Kayla wondered how she was going to heat up Mia's bottle. They knew the baby did not like it cold.

Joshua was dressed as he came into the living room. "Stay inside. There are power lines in the yard. I've got to go check on the others and see if everyone is all right."

Staring up at him, she wanted to kiss him again; she was so worried about his safety. "You be careful. I'm going to see if Eugenia can show me how to cook over a fire in the fireplace."

The ghost turned and laughed. "I would love to. We're going to need to heat up Mia a bottle soon."

"Yes," Kayla said as she turned to Joshua. "You're going to check on your cousins? Aunt Rose?"

"Yes," he said, putting on his work boots. In the semi-darkness, he appeared concerned.

"If I can help with anything, come and get me. I hope everyone is all right," she said worried about them.

Joshua reached out and touched her arm, and heat exploded inside her like a bomb. She gazed at him, wondering if he felt the same attraction.

"There's no way I'm going to let you out there. We have a generator somewhere, so we'll be setting up someplace with power until we can get ours restored. I'll take you over in the golf cart, if we still have one, to the clubhouse. We may all be living there until we get power back."

When he opened the front door, his cousins Travis and Tanner were walking up the steps.

"You guys okay?" Travis asked.

"Yes, how about you?"

"Other than losing ten years off my life, we're good," Travis said. "I was sleeping so good when Samantha woke me up and said the storm had gotten worse. We barely made it into the closet before it hit."

"I thought I was back in Afghanistan," Tanner said. "But Emily managed to get me into the closet where she sang to me, bringing me back. When was the last time we had a storm that bad?"

This was news to Kayla and she wondered if Tanner had PTSD.

"Can't remember. But when I saw the transformers blowing and the funnel in the light flashes, I knew what was happening," Joshua said.

The men sighed. "We all spent the night in the closet. I wonder about the others," Travis said.

"Let's go check on them," Joshua replied.

The men walked away and Kayla couldn't help but gaze out the window at the destruction.

Even the guard shack was lying in the road, a pile of broken lumber. Big electric trucks rumbled onto the ranch and she sighed with relief. "Great. They're already here to restore power."

"What does that mean?" Eugenia asked.

"That means soon everything will come back on if they can get it fixed. I'm sure there are blown transformers everywhere."

Her cell phone dinged and she glanced at it. Joshua had sent her a text.

Just checking to see if I can reach you by cell.

Yes, she replied. *Be careful.*

Staring at the message, mixed emotions filled her. Last night, when they thought they were going to die, his kiss had been filled with passion and desire, and the urge to give herself to him was strong.

But she had to remember they had different desires for life.

Still in her pajamas, she went into the kitchen knowing that soon the baby would want her bottle. She found a pot and filled it with water, then she went into the living room and started the gas logs. She couldn't use the automatic starter, but she could light the flame herself.

Now they would have heat and hopefully soon Mia would have warm formula. Maybe she'd even fix herself a cup of tea.

"You could have been a pioneer," Eugenia told her. "Is there a rod you can hang to put the pot on?"

"Yes," she said, excited. Soon she had the water heating. Then she went in and changed Mia.

When the water was boiling, she made herself some tea and put the baby's bottle in the water to heat.

Just as she sat down to feed Mia, there was a knock on her door.

"Come in," she called out and Samantha poked her head in. She saw the ghost.

"Hi, Eugenia," she said.

Mia's mouth dropped open. "You two know each other," Kayla asked. Why did she think the matchmaking ghost was only her friend?

"Yes, since Samantha was a girl, we've been friends."

That was a while ago.

"She's matched three of the Burnett men, including me and Travis," Samantha said. "If not for her, I'd be back in New York searching for a job in television."

That was good to know. What were the odds that she was trying to do the same to her and Joshua?

"Did your house sustain any damage?" Kayla asked.

"Don't know yet, but Travis thinks we'll need a new roof," she said. "You probably will too."

Kayla wished she could offer her some refreshments, but she didn't have much that she didn't have to heat. "Would you like some hot tea?"

"Yes," Samantha said.

The woman's baby bump was now showing prominently with her due in a little over two months. She sank down onto a chair.

Mia started to cry and Kayla glanced at the baby. "Just a minute and your breakfast will be ready."

"Can I feed her?" Samantha asked.

"Sure," Kayla said and picked up Mia and took her to the woman.

She handed her the bottle and the woman sighed with pleasure. "Two more months and our little one will be here."

"I'll show you the nursery later," Kayla told her as she fixed the tea.

Kayla had been so confused all morning. After spending most of the night in the closet with Joshua, she didn't know what to do. They had kissed not once, but several times, and he'd touched her breast.

What was she doing?

It was like once they kissed under the mistletoe, they had wanted to continue. When they feared for their life, they had kissed in the closet for a long time. When you thought you might die, you threw out your concerns and concentrated on the moment.

"You guys shared quite the kiss under the mistletoe last night," Samantha said.

Eugenia perked up. "What? Where?"

"At our house. Joshua kissed Kayla under the mistletoe," Samantha said with a laugh. "It was quite a kiss."

They could have kept that a secret from Eugenia. She didn't need to know how their first kiss went down.

"Thanks for sharing," Kayla said.

The ghost laughed. "You're just confirming my beliefs."

"Has Eugenia been trying to match the two of you, yet?" Samantha asked.

Kayla turned to Eugenia and smiled. "Yes, she gave me all the reasons I needed the Burnetts and how they needed me. How Joshua is really a good man."

Samantha smiled.

"Travis lost his first wife and child due to a drunk driver. He was never going to marry again and then I showed up. Sometimes men say one thing and they do the exact opposite."

"Joshua is my employer," Kayla said. "I can't get involved with him."

Though that had not stopped her last night. In fact, just thinking about the man, heat spread through her. If only he wanted to give up his single life, but she was almost certain he missed going out every night.

Samantha glanced down at Mia and smiled. The baby was sucking on her bottle, making soft little noises and enjoying her breakfast. "You're in a precarious position. I think Joshua is a good man and just is on the wrong path. I think you and Mia can help him to see he's not living a sustainable lifestyle.

A different woman or dating several women at the same time, that can't last forever."

Maybe not, but would Joshua see it that way?

"He's been home more since you and Mia have been here than ever before. Normally he would be out almost every night. You're good for him."

"Thanks," Kayla said, wondering if she could fall for another man like David. And yet, Joshua was different. She liked the way he tried to take care of her and Mia. Last night in the closet with the tornado roaring not far from them, he'd crawled on top of both of them to protect them if the roof caved in or the tornado tried to suck them up.

At night, he enjoyed his time with Mia and she could see they were forming a bond. A bond he needed to encourage with his daughter.

The way he was learning to give Mia a bath, fix her formula, and even change her diapers, said he had a chance of being a good father. But what if he decided not to keep her, give her to her grandparents? Could she accept that decision?

Never.

Eugenia had been shimmering in the corner listening to them. "You modern girls, I don't know what to think of you. Kayla, sweetheart, you are the one for Joshua. He needs you and you need him. What is it going to take to make the both of you realize that you're meant for one another?"

"Why do you say this?"

"Because I can see the way the two of you glance at each other. There is enough sizzle between you to heat this house."

Kayla frowned. "I'm not going to accept him being a womanizer. I will not accept him cheating on me. I'm not going to accept him dating other women besides me. If he wants to settle down, I'm worth it, but I want a man who loves me and is not going to just use me to take care of his daughter. If he's for me, then he has to show me he loves me."

After the last fiasco, she would not accept any man who didn't understand about her being a foster child. Of not knowing where her family was located.

"But you are attracted to him?" Samantha asked.

Why were they forcing her to say this out loud? She didn't want to admit that she found Joshua so damn attractive. She didn't want to think about how she had spent the night kissing him in the closet.

"Yes," she finally said.

The ghost and Samantha glanced at one another. "Well, that was like pulling teeth."

"It's a difficult situation. I'm his employee. I'm taking care of his daughter," she said, gazing at the sweet bundle in Samantha's arms. "He has to want me for me."

"You're right," Samantha said.

Too much had happened in the last twenty-four hours and Kayla wasn't ready to share her secrets with these women. For that matter, she hadn't shared everything with Joshua.

"Ladies, how will this affect Christmas at the ranch? Joshua told me the family gathers on Christmas Day and everyone spends Christmas Eve with their immediate family. Do you think that will change?"

Eugenia shook her head. "You're changing the subject."

"You're right, I am," she said. "What happens between me and Joshua is between us. Not anyone else, even the match-making ghost."

CHAPTER 16

*T*hat night when Joshua came home, he was tired. They were lucky to have dodged one hundred-mile-an-hour winds. It had been a small tornado and yet the damage it caused was monumental.

One side of the main road through the ranch was a complete mess. The other side, his side, had slight damage. The barns had lost most of their roofs and the guard shack was in splinters.

Already his Aunt Rose had filed a report with their insurance company. After Christmas, most of the homes on the property would be receiving new roofs. They had lost at least twenty-five head of cattle. The swimming pool was filled with debris that no one wanted to climb in and clean out.

Even the thought of the cold water had him shivering.

Most of all, he couldn't stop thinking about how Mia and Kayla were under his protection. His care. And they could all have died.

Standing inside the door, he noticed that Mia was sitting

in her swing waving her hands and cooing. The baby was happy. What if last night she'd died in the tornado?

Kayla was in the kitchen cooking. Thank goodness they had gotten the power back on fairly easily.

The house was filled with a delicious smell and fear smacked him in the gut. This must be what being married and in a happy home felt like.

Coming home to a cheerful baby and his wife cooking dinner. But not his parents' home. When he came home from school, his mother would be sitting on the couch watching television, his father was working. When his father got home, his mother had often left to go to the country club and there was no dinner cooked.

Not unless his father made the meal.

"I'm going to take a shower," he told Kayla.

"Go ahead," she said.

In his bedroom, he shut the door and stripped. Standing under the warm spray of the shower, the events of the last twenty-four hours seemed to overpower him. He leaned his arm against the shower wall and let the water hit him in the face.

What was he doing? They could have all been killed last night and there wasn't anything he could have done to stop the roof from blowing off and the tornado lifting them out and flinging them into the next county.

How did one stop caring about people who were depending on you? Wasn't that one of the reasons he said he would never marry? He didn't want to disappoint anyone like his mother had devastated her children. How many times had she hurt him and his brothers by not being there when she said she would be? Birthdays, graduations, special occasions, holidays. They meant nothing to her.

Getting out of the shower, he dried off and wrapped a towel around him. He went to the mirror to comb his wet hair.

The smell of lavender swirled around him and Eugenia shimmered behind him.

"Eugenia, a little privacy would be nice," he said, thinking how she would feel if he dropped the towel around his waist.

The ghost ignored him.

"There was nothing you could have done," she said.

Frowning, he couldn't help but wonder how the ghost knew what he was thinking. Did she know how frightened he'd been when he saw all the damage and knew they were so lucky that his house was on the other side of the main drive?

"Are you a mind reader as well?"

"No, but I could see the panic-stricken expression on your face. Stop. You protected them the best you could have last night."

"Well, it wasn't good enough. I'm talking to a storm expert tomorrow and we're going to put a cellar or a protected room in the house. When you feel the house shaking and you think you're about to die, the storm is too close."

The woman smiled at him. "That's a smart idea. I kept telling Thomas we needed a storm cellar and he wouldn't listen. Said by the time we got to it, the tornado would have blown us away. But it would be a way to protect your wife and baby."

Joshua could feel his body tense. "Wife? Who the hell said I was getting married?"

"Now, Joshua," Eugenia said. "You see how happy your cousins are. Your daughter needs a mother. You can't let your past keep you from finding happiness."

Happiness, his ass.

His past was what kept him dating women who just liked to be his sex toy and nothing else. And yet there was no deep friendship. No sense in trying to figure out what that person was thinking or feeling. Nothing serious. Only a gratification that he felt between his legs, nothing more.

And that was the scary part as well. Look how frightened he'd become over Kayla's safety last night. If he didn't care about the person in his bed, then he would have felt bad, but not devastated. Losing Kayla and Mia would have wrecked him.

And feeling that way had him terrified.

He had enjoyed Kayla's company these last few weeks. And yet the thought of marriage would have him racing his truck to the next county. The memory of his mother. The divorce. The weekends standing outside waiting, and her never show-ing up.

The way his family seemed to disintegrate right before his eyes. He couldn't go through that kind of thing again.

"My past keeps me from a lot of things," he said, combing his hair. "My past is what sends me running to the bars to escape the memories of our happy home."

Eugenia sighed and shook her head. "Darling, your mother was not the greatest, but you've turned out to be a good man."

"Oh yeah," he said. "Ask Skylar, Judy, Beth, or any other of the girls that call here on a regular basis. I'm just their moment-of-need man, that's all. They know better than to think of marrying me, and maybe Kayla needs to understand that as much as I'd like to be her moment-of-need man, she would hate me in the end. So stop trying to matchmake us, Eugenia. Not happening."

The ghost shook her head vehemently.

"Ask Travis, Tanner, or Tucker. You Burnett men are all the same, only you each have your own set of problems when it comes to women. All of you want the sex but nothing else. My sons never intended to get married, but how do you think you got here? You are here because of my son Tanner, and believe me, we had to get him out of trouble before he could marry. You remind me a lot of him. You're a direct descendent."

Why was she carrying on about her son? Did she think he cared? Since Mia's arrival, he'd become soft, but the hardass was still in him, and he was about to let him out to create havoc and set things right.

After last night, it was time for the ghost to vacate the building.

"Eugenia, your son has been dead for close to one hundred years," he said. "Maybe I came from his lineage, but I'm my own man. Now this towel wrapped around my waist is about to be dropped. So I suggest you shimmy on out of here unless you want to see my junk."

"Your what? Has the male anatomy changed?"

Junk was obviously not in her vocabulary. "No, it hasn't changed. But unless you want me to embarrass you, it's time to go. I'll give you a three-second countdown. One, two…"

Suddenly she swished out of the room, and he sighed. "If you don't leave the house, I'm calling a ghost hunter."

"You all say that," she said. "Go ahead. I'll scare the man into his grave."

Damn, she was calling his bluff.

Five minutes later, he walked into the dining room just as Kayla put their plates on the table.

She glanced up at him, her blonde hair pulled back. What would it feel like to run his hands through her hair and pull those pink cherry lips to his again?

Stop! He had to stop thinking of her as a woman, but rather his nanny.

"Are you ready to eat?"

"Yes," he said, gazing at her full lips, the memory of their kiss sending his blood heating. He needed to remember that he was not the kind of man she wanted. He was every relationship-seeking woman's worst nightmare.

As they sat, she glanced at him and he could see the questions in her eyes. It was best he pretended that he didn't see she wanted to discuss what was happening to them. He couldn't talk to her, not without making her mad. And she took damn good care of Mia. Right now, he needed her more than ever with all the work to be done around the ranch.

Taking a bite, she glanced across the table at him. Never before had it felt awkward between them, but right now, he wanted to jump up and run.

"How much damage is there?"

"A lot," he said, glancing down at his plate. "Most of the guest cottages are going to need new roofs and even some repairs. One cottage may not be salvageable. We'll have to let the insurance company decide what to do."

She sighed and he could see her gaze questioning. "Are you too tired to watch Mia this evening?"

He was, but he was not about to give up time with his daughter. And it would put a buffer between the two of them.

"No," he said.

"Do we have internet?"

"I don't know," he said, wondering what she was doing on the internet. He'd seen the old computer she had and wondered how it even still operated.

It was then he knew what he was going to get her for Christmas. It was then that he realized he wanted to give her something special.

He didn't know why she spent most evenings on the computer, but it was none of his business, and yet he knew how he could help her.

"How is your aunt Rose?"

The conversation he'd had this afternoon with Aunt Rose was enough to send him running out the gate. The old woman didn't understand why all the damage couldn't be repaired in a week and why it would cost them so much money.

Lumber was the highest it had ever been, and materials, in general, were scarce and this storm had not helped that situation.

Aunt Rose was so tight, it was a wonder she didn't squeak when she walked.

"Not happy," he said. "Why can't we get the ranch repaired now? What is going to take so long? Why is it so expensive? Maybe we should all work through Christmas."

"It's next week," she said. "Does Aunt Rose realize how soon the holiday will be here? We need to talk about what we're getting Mia for Christmas. Do you have decorations? I could put up the tree."

"No," he said. "A single man doesn't need decorations."

He'd never in his life decorated for Christmas. As a young boy, he remembered his mother decorating, but in the years after she left, there had been nothing.

"Well, I enjoy them and Mia will find them delightful," she said. "And she needs a Christmas gift from Santa."

Santa? Really? His mother had never believed in giving gifts from Santa. The memory made him even crankier.

"How is Mia going to know about lights and decorations and what they're for? And Santa? She's going on four months old. The child doesn't need Santa."

Kayla was quiet for a moment. "Suit yourself. I just thought it would be nice to have a little Christmas cheer around here. I'll clean up the dishes and then I'm taking my evening off." She stood, taking her dishes to the sink.

He'd been an ass to her and yet he couldn't apologize because then things would be happier between them, and he was too busy constructing walls between himself and the nanny.

Mia started to cry. He picked her up.

"What's wrong?"

She wailed and he reached down and felt a wet diaper and then he smelled a rank scent.

"Thanks, Mia," he said as he carried her into the nursery and placed her on the changing table. When he set her down, he saw the baby poop on his shirt. The damn diaper leaked and she had poop all over her clothes, running down her leg and even on him.

She would need a complete change.

A gag hit him so hard that he choked trying to keep from throwing up. He wanted to yell to Kayla to come help him, but she was not happy with him and it would be better if he avoided her.

"Mia, I'm tired. I had to work hard today. Now Kayla is angry at me and you're pooping on me. Give me a break."

Her bottom lip trembled and he lifted her legs and took a baby wipe to her. He was a single man. What in the hell was he doing cleaning up baby poop?

Why wasn't he out in bars having a good time? Searching for an eligible woman who he could take home for the night?

Instead he was wiping poop off his shirt.

What was Kayla doing on the computer? Suddenly he wanted her by his side, talking to him, making faces at Mia. Hell, he'd buy her and the kid all the Christmas decorations and toys for Mia that she wanted. But he wanted Kayla close.

She felt nice and snug against his body, her breasts crushed against his chest.

He wanted to smell her instead of Mia.

And damn, he wanted to taste those full lips of hers that were beckoning to him.

What the hell was he going to do? He wanted what he couldn't have and that frustrated him.

CHAPTER 17

*T*wo days later, Kayla was changing Mia when Joshua walked into the house three hours early.

She knew it was him because of the way his boots sounded on the wooden floor.

He walked into the nursery. Since the tornado, he'd been polite, yet curt. And she feared he regretted kissing her. They had not spoken about what happened in the closet and seemed to pretend it never happened.

But she knew they both remembered that night.

Every night he'd come in exhausted, and yet each night, he made time for Mia. Most men would have said *I'm too tired*, but not Josh.

"Get ready, we're leaving," he said, standing in the doorway, his brilliant blue eyes gazing at her. "Dress Mia warmly."

"Where are we going?" she asked, wondering where he was taking her and the baby.

Shaking his head, he smiled at her. "It's a surprise."

It was three days before Christmas and she had been

feeling down. This would be a good excuse to get out. Maybe it would cheer her up.

The baby smiled and laughed at her and that made her heart sing with love for the child. This little girl continued to bring her joy and reminded her that someday she'd have a daughter of her own. Someday.

She bundled her up and handed the baby to Joshua. "Give me just a moment to grab my coat."

Hurrying into her room, she pulled a fresh sweater over her head and then put a dab of lipstick on. Maybe it would keep him from kissing her again if she had lipstick on her lips.

Anything to put a barrier between them.

Grabbing her coat and purse she hurried out the door.

When they were all in Joshua's truck, he glanced at her and she could feel his blue eyes staring at her.

"I'm sorry if I've been a little moody the last few days," he said.

Shocked that he was apologizing, she turned to face him. "I thought it was the kiss in the closet. I thought you regretted what we did."

"Partly. More than anything, I couldn't stop thinking about that tornado being so close and not being able to protect the two of you. After seeing all the damage, I was frightened at how close we came. And yes, that kiss still haunts me at night."

"Good," she said. "I'm glad it's not just me."

A smile crossed his face at her admission to her reaction to his kiss. While she liked the fact that he wanted to protect the two of them, he wasn't responsible for her well-being.

"You're not liable for me," she said. "If I died in that tornado, it would have been God's will and there would've been nothing you could've done to stop it. Yes, I was frightened, but you were doing your best to protect us. That's all we can ask for."

He turned back toward the wheel of the truck and watched the road.

"Christmas has never been my favorite time of year," he said. "My parents never did much for Christmas. We didn't have Santa. Most of the time, we didn't even put up a tree. It was just another day unless Dad took us over to the Burnetts'."

She could see the pain on his face. He'd made several references to his family not being the best, and yet he had all his cousins, a large family. How did that sit with the other Burnetts?

"What about your cousins? Didn't you spend time with them?"

With a sigh, he laughed. "Occasionally, but mother hated the Burnetts. When she was around, she kept us all away from them. We didn't live on the ranch until she left. Then my father moved us to one of the family homes and he worked for them again. Until his death."

That explained why his situation was different. "Why would your mother hate the Burnetts? Don't you all receive dividends? It's a big operation."

She couldn't imagine hating the family. They seemed to get along great.

"Yes, but mother's family was high society, and well, we're not known for being into attending a lot of social functions. We're just a working ranch that has a few oil wells and a dude ranch."

That was hard for Kayla to comprehend. When you came

from the foster care system, you concentrated on whether or not your new family would have enough food to eat. Whether or not you had decent clothes to wear.

"You would think your mother would make a big deal of Christmas," she said. "That her kids would be spoiled."

He laughed. "Our cousins were. They would get the latest toys. We were told that our presents were donated to needy children."

"Well, that was nice," Kayla told him, wondering if she had ever received one of his donated gifts.

"Yes, but it would have been fun to open presents under the tree," he said.

She could understand him feeling that way.

"You have a daughter. Maybe you should start your own thing," she said. "Don't do what your family did, but start your own Christmas traditions."

A smile crossed his face. "You're right. And that begins today."

She hoped this meant he was going to keep Mia. That he had decided not to give the little girl to her grandparents.

"Oh?"

"We're on our way to buy a Christmas tree and all the decorations," he said. "Then we'll swing by the store and get something from Santa. My daughter is going to enjoy Christmas and have presents and a visit from Santa. We'll also give something to needy children in her name."

Kayla smiled at him. "That's a wonderful idea."

"If it's late when we return, maybe we can take her Christmas light looking," she said.

"What's that?"

Her jaw dropped open; she couldn't believe he'd never been Christmas light looking.

"You drive around neighborhoods and look at people's decorations. Some neighborhoods go all out and it's so much fun to see what people have done," she said.

Those were her happiest memories of Christmas. She'd learned early not to expect presents and she never asked for what she wanted because most of the families had other children and their needs came before her own.

But the worst memory of Christmas was last year. Only by the grace of God had she survived.

Quickly, she pushed the thought out of her mind. Today, she didn't want to remember last year. Today was about giving Joshua and Mia a good Christmas experience.

"That would be fun," Joshua said. "Do you think she'll be awake?"

"We'll see," she said. "She's staying awake longer now between her naps."

They pulled into the Christmas tree lot.

"I've never bought a tree before," Joshua said, glancing at her.

She smiled. "It's not hard. Come on, it will be fun."

Kayla stepped out of the truck and Joshua brought the stroller over they had purchased.

She lifted the baby out of the car seat and tucked her into the stroller. It was her first outing in the little buggy and she gazed around while Kayla strapped her in. Then she put a blanket around her to keep her warm.

It wasn't really cold, but she didn't want her to get sick. Standing, she smiled at Joshua. "Come on, let's go get a tree."

They walked through the aisles of fresh trees and Joshua gazed around, pushing the stroller.

"Who knew there were so many different kinds."

"Yes," she said, grinning.

"Pick one out," he said.

"No, we have to choose one that we both like. I'll give you several examples and then you decide which one. But, first, where are you going to put the tree?"

He shrugged. "I don't know. It can't block the television and I don't want it near a heater vent. We don't want it drying out too quickly and catching fire."

She pulled one out and twirled it around. "What about this one? It's tall, but not too tall that it takes up the whole room."

"Looks good," Joshua said. He leaned down to Mia. "What do you think, princess? It's your first Christmas tree."

She smiled at him and then she farted.

"Oh no," he said.

Kayla laughed. "It's okay. I brought the bag. It's in the truck."

"What all do we need?"

Just then a man walked up. "You folks in search of a tree?"

"This one," Kayla said.

"All right. Do you want me to cut the end of it off or leave it like it is?"

"No, cut the end off," she said, knowing the trunk would soak up more water that way. "Where are your stands?"

"Up front. I'll meet you up there," he said.

Joshua hung back and watched the man cut off the end of the tree and then he put it on a machine that netted the branches. "Wow, I didn't know so much went into purchasing a tree."

"Oh just wait. We're not done yet," Kayla said.

When they went to the front, the man carried the tree up to the register. "Here you go."

Kayla then picked out a stand, lights, and several boxes of ornaments. "Oh, and we need either an angel or a star to put on top," she said. "Which do you want?" She found both and held them up.

"I don't care," he said. "Let Mia choose."

The baby was staring at all the decorations.

"Which one, Mia," he told her. "Blow a raspberry if you want the Angel and fart if you want the star."

Kayla laughed. "That's not nice."

"Well, how else do you know her decision," he said.

She stepped up to the child and knelt in front of her. "Which one do you want?"

The baby cooed and then tried to grab the angel.

"The angel it is," she said. "And that is how you do it."

Rising, she smiled at Joshua and noticed how dark his eyes had become. It was like they suddenly filled with passion. She glanced at his lips, remembering the way they tasted. The feel of them moving across her own, the way her breath became short.

Quickly she glanced away.

"Come on, Mr. Burnett," she said, trying to put a safe space between them. "We need to find a tree skirt and then we're done," she told him. "Next up, toys."

Joshua paid for all the decorations and they climbed back

in the truck. Kayla buckled the baby in the car seat and soon they were on their way to the baby store.

When they walked in, the same clerk that had helped them last time was working.

"You had your baby," she said, running over to them. "She's so cute."

Kayla didn't know what to say.

"Oh, she looks like her mother," the clerk said.

Did the woman not remember that she wasn't pregnant the last time they were there? Yes, they had spent a huge amount of money, but that didn't mean they were expecting.

"Thanks," Joshua said and pushed the baby buggy past the girl. He grumbled under his breath.

Kayla loved seeing the womanizer pushing the stroller.

When they had walked off, he shook his head. "That was rude."

"She doesn't know our situation," Kayla said and thought of her own baby. She pushed the thought out of her mind.

"What are we going to buy Miss Mia," she said.

Joshua shrugged. "I don't know enough about what babies like. You decide."

"No, we're going to pick it out together," Kayla told him. "You're her father and I'm just her nanny."

He stopped in the store. "Don't say that. You've taken care of her and shown her more love than anyone. Probably even more than her mother."

Confusion swirled in her. The man was fighting his attraction to her, and yet he didn't want her to be considered just the nanny.

"But that's all I am," she said softly. "Believe me, I love this little girl and would die protecting her, but at the end of the day, I'm just her nanny. You, you're her father."

With a sigh, he pushed the baby stroller again. The looks from the women in the store, seeing this handsome man push the stroller were almost comical.

"Come on," he said, growling. "Let's get her some Santa toys and get home."

Just then Mia let out a squeal. They both glanced to make certain she was all right. It was then that Kayla saw the tall stuffed pink giraffe. Her bright blue eyes were staring at the stuffed animal and her hands were waving in the air.

"Do you think she wants the giraffe," Joshua asked.

"I don't know, but something caused her to squeal."

They rolled her up close to the stuffed animal and she kicked her legs and squealed with pleasure.

"I think we've found what Santa is bringing Miss Mia," Kayla said.

"That is something I would never have picked out," Joshua said.

"Me either," Kayla said with a smile. "Now let's get her a few more things and I think we're done. Then we can go home and put it all together."

Mia was starting to get drowsy, and soon she'd want her bottle and to go to bed.

Ten minutes later, they had several educational-type of baby toys and were on their way to the checkout.

"Do you want to get something to eat?" Joshua asked her.

"That would be nice, but I think we need to get Mia home. It's getting close to her bedtime and she'll be fussy."

With a sigh, he nodded. "Babies certainly know how to throw a wrench in your plans."

Kayla smiled. "Yes, they do. And just think, she'll be in your life forever and under your roof for the next eighteen years."

They rolled out of the store with a cart full of toys that Joshua pushed while Kayla pushed the stroller.

When they reached the truck, Kayla locked the stroller next to the truck and helped him unload all the toys they'd bought.

Joshua went to the stroller and lifted the baby and put her in her seat and buckled her in. When he went to turn around, Kayla was standing right behind him, watching to make certain he had her safely buckled in.

They were inches apart and he bumped into her. He grabbed her by the shoulders to keep her from falling and she gazed up at him. Licking her lips, she felt the weight of his hands on her shoulders and she wanted to lean into him and soak up his essence.

His mouth lowered to hers and she relaxed against him. At first, it was a reluctant kiss, but then it gathered steam. His lips were demanding and insistent, and she moaned at the feel of his tongue as it swept across her mouth. He smelled of soap and man, and she could feel his cock pressed into her center and she wanted more.

Suddenly he released her and stepped away.

"Let's go," he said. "We can't be out here making out in the parking lot. We've got a Christmas tree to decorate."

Kayla touched her lips and wondered if they were back to making out or if he had a moment of weakness.

CHAPTER 18

$\mathcal{I}$t was Christmas Eve and Joshua had never felt more excited about the holiday than he did today. He'd managed to sneak off and purchase a new laptop for Kayla and even bought his daughter a couple of new dresses.

Little girls loved fashion and knowing how crazy her mother had been about having the latest style, he expected Mia would be that way too. And he just felt so good about buying her something.

Something from her father.

If someone had told him he would be taking care of a baby and not out at the bars every night, he would have laughed at them and told them they were crazy. But this week marked three weeks that Mia had been with him, and he had enjoyed every moment.

But even more, he enjoyed Kayla. The woman completely different from the women he picked up at bars. And he liked that she was not like the others.

His normal bar woman was as fake as they came, but Kayla

was normal. She was more down to earth. And she looked beautiful with or without makeup. She was natural and he was amazed how attracted he was to her.

When Kayla was not around, he snuck the packages under the tree. His very first real Christmas tree and he loved the smell in the house. Sure, his mother had a big fancy tree that glittered, but she'd never let the boys decorate it because they would not make it perfect.

But this tree, he and Kayla had decorated and he'd enjoyed seeing the lights sparkle in her eyes. The way they ran the lights around, laughing, and then hung the glass balls.

It was an experience he would always remember – the jokes they made, the happiness that seemed to radiate from Kayla, the warmth he felt around her.

The Beal family would be home in two days, and at that time, he would be forced to make a decision. Right now, he felt more confused than ever. God, how he wanted to keep Mia, but then he would think of everything he was missing out on and wonder if he was making the right choice for himself.

After all, he'd sworn to never marry or have children, and yet here he was a father.

The smell of lavender filled the room.

"You need to go to the kitchen," Eugenia told him, shimmering in front of him.

"Why? Is the house on fire," he said, heading to the door.

"No, but go," she said.

Glancing back at the ghost, he shook his head and walked into the kitchen.

Mia was napping in her swing. A cup of hot tea along with

freshly baked Christmas cookies that he had every intention of taking a bite of sat on the counter. Nothing seemed out of the ordinary, but then he heard the sobs.

Gut-wrenching sobs came from Kayla's bedroom.

Glancing at the closed door, the smell of lavender permeated the room and the door suddenly opened for him.

"Kayla, sweetheart, are you all right?"

He'd never been one to comfort a woman and yet he couldn't take the sound of her crying and not find out what was wrong.

Maybe she'd received some kind of bad news. He realized then, he knew nothing about her family while she knew everything about his. Since she'd been staying with him, she had never mentioned her mother or father or if she even had any brothers and sisters.

It was Christmas Eve, shouldn't they have called or texted her? Shouldn't she be somewhere besides the Burnett Ranch taking care of his daughter?

"Get out," she said and turned her face away, her shoulders shaking as she cried her heart out.

Something was wrong. Very wrong.

He felt almost a push toward her and glanced back to see Eugenia pointing at the bed, mouthing the words *go to her*.

She wanted to be alone, and yet he couldn't leave her like this.

Sinking on the bed, he lay down beside her and rolled her to him. He pulled her into his arms. "Kayla, tell me what's wrong."

Shaking her head, he felt her sobbing against his chest.

"Did someone die?" She nodded and tried to control the sobs that made her shake. "Who?"

"My baby," she said quietly. "One year ago today."

Astonished, he held her tightly. To someone like Kayla, the death of her child would be the end of her world. And now he understood why she would feel that way. If something happened to Mia, he'd be devastated.

"What happened," he asked her.

"I'm sorry," she said. "I didn't expect this to hit me so hard today, but it was like all the feelings of being alone came rushing back."

"Where was the father?"

She gave a little laugh.

"David didn't want our child. As soon as he found out I was pregnant, he ended the relationship and his father fired me. Told me to get an abortion, that they weren't paying child support."

That was cold. Damn cold.

He pulled her in closer to his chest and held her there.

"He's a classless dick," he said. "You should have sued them."

"No, I'm going to slowly steal all their clients from them," she said, wiping away her tears.

Glancing at her, he frowned. "How are you going to do that?"

"I'm creating my own marketing company. There are clients at Frantz Marketing Firm that I brought to the company. Clients that I worked very closely with to get their business. They've already lost two. My plan is to get every client I brought to their company to follow me. To work with me. I know their needs, they don't."

It was a smart strategy.

"Is that what you do every night on the computer?"

"Yes," she said, sniffing. "Today was the day I miscarried, and every time I've looked at Mia today, I've wondered what my baby would look like. It's been so hard."

He pulled her in closer again as the tears rolled down her face.

"Were you alone when you miscarried or did David come to your side?" he asked needing to understand.

"No, I was alone," she said. "I drove myself to the ER."

With a sigh, he wanted to walk out of this house and find that son of a bitch and kick his ass into next week. The man was a complete bastard for the way he'd treated Kayla.

And Kayla was the strongest woman he'd ever met to have gone through a miscarriage alone.

Yet, Joshua wondered if he had known that Skylar was pregnant, how he would've treated her. Would he have been such a dick? And sadly, a year ago, he feared that he might have been.

Today, he realized he would be different, but a year ago, no.

"There is nothing I can say that will make you feel better," he told her, holding her close. "You've experienced a loss that I can't comprehend. I'm just sorry that there was no one there to help you get through that terrible time."

She squeezed him. "Thank you. I've been alone most of my life. I'm used to taking care of myself."

Her words surprised him. His life had been unusual,

different, but he'd always had his brothers, cousins, and even Aunt Rose who would sneak the boys things their mother refused to let them have.

"What do you mean you've always been alone?"

Lying on his chest, she gave a little sob. "The reason David's father didn't want him to marry me is because I'm a foster child. CPS picked me up when I was twelve. I'd been living alone for a week and the neighbors finally called them."

Shock filled Joshua.

"Since you were twelve, you'd been in foster care?"

"Yes," she said. "I got a new family about every two years. You quickly learned not to say much when you first arrived, but to learn the family dynamics before you acted yourself around people. Sometimes they accepted who you were, but other times, they tried to change you. I grew up with three different families."

He couldn't imagine.

"Do you ever hear from any of them?"

She laughed. "No. The last family let me stay until I started college, but after that, I never went back. The state paid for my college education, but I had to work to buy my books and dorm fees."

He remembered how they kicked everyone out of the dorms during the summer. He'd never imagined not having a place to go to during the off months.

"What did you do during the summer?"

"I tried to line up staying a couple of weeks each year with my friends until I could get back in the dorm. The last year, I had a good-paying job and used the money to stay in a hotel for two months."

He couldn't fathom how hard life had been on Kayla.

"Do you know anything about where your parents are?"

She shook her head. "My father, I never knew. My mother left one day and never returned. I did my best to hide in that house, but one of the neighbors saw the lights on one night and she hadn't seen my mother's car. She came over the next morning and I told her I was fine, but later that day CPS showed up and took me away."

All the money that Joshua had been blessed with made him feel guilty. Who did this to their child? He glanced at Mia still sleeping in the swing. No matter what, he would never let CPS take her from him.

"I had an excellent life after college. Working for Frantz Marketing Firm, I had a good salary. Two years after starting there, I saved enough money to purchase a nice condo. Drove a great car, and when I got pregnant, I was thrilled. Soon, I would have my own family. Children with the man I thought I loved. But little did I know he was dating some rich socialite his father wanted him to marry. I was just his temporary girl."

Guilt filled Joshua and he wondered if he had ever been so cruel to a woman before. Had he been like her David?

She gave a little laugh. "The foster child wasn't good enough for the boss's son."

Now Joshua really wanted to kick David's ass.

"Why didn't you get another marketing job?"

"George Frantz blacklisted me in the city of Dallas. I would have had to move out of state. At the time, I needed a break and I had always enjoyed taking care of the foster babies. So I decided it would be good for me to become a nanny, and at night, work on my business plan."

This woman was incredible. She'd managed to outwit the Frantzs, and soon, he knew she would take many of their clients. And he would do everything he could to help her. Even give her money if she needed it to start her business.

"You have survived so much. Why didn't I know this about you before now?"

"Would you tell your prospective boss that the last company you worked for blackballed you? What if you don't think I'm a good person because I was raised by foster families? You have to be careful who you tell."

Lifting her face, he stared into her emerald eyes. "No. Don't ever be ashamed of who you are. You're smart, brave, and beautiful."

Tears welled in her eyes. "And yet one year ago today, I lost everything."

"You're going to come back stronger than ever," he said as he stared at her full lips wanting to kiss them.

Why this woman? Why Kayla?

His cock pulsed with need for her, but right now, all she needed was for him to hold her.

Just then Mia made a little squealing noise to let them know she was awake. They both grinned at each other. She squealed a little louder. On the third attempt, she poked her bottom lip out and began to wail.

"I think the princess needs a diaper change and a bottle," Kayla said.

She moved across the bed to the floor, but then she stopped and glanced back.

"Thank you, Joshua. Thank you for making me feel better. This day will always be hard, but you made it a little easier."

141

She picked up the infant and he sat there watching the sway of her hips glide away.

An ache filled him. No, his childhood had not been easy, but damn, it had not been near as hard as hers.

The woman deserved so much. And God, how he wanted her. And he wanted to fulfill all her dreams and give her everything she deserved.

CHAPTER 19

*L*ater that night, they were putting the toys they had bought Mia under the tree. Joshua sat by the tree, reading the instructions on how to put together a baby walker.

"I think they deliberately write this in a way that no one can understand," he said. "It's like it's written in Greek."

She smiled at him as she wrapped a couple of gifts he had bought for the family Christmas.

She held up a beautiful leather coat. "Who did you buy this for?"

"Aunt Rose," he said. "In this family, you always get the monarch something nice for Christmas. Though what she needs and what she gets is completely different."

She smiled. After crying all afternoon, the tears were right below the surface. It was like once she started, it was hard to stop. And the thought of having an aunt that led the family was so foreign to her. She would have loved to have been part of this huge family.

"Who is this for?" she asked, holding up what appeared to be three faces that were planters.

"We're having an as-seen-on-TV exchange," he said. "We play a Christmas game where people can steal your gift. It's all in fun."

For a moment, she didn't say anything. Why she had expected him to ask her to attend his family Christmas, she didn't know. She would spend the day watching wonderful Christmas stories on television and dreaming of how, if she ever had her own family, they would spend the holidays.

She wrapped the gifts and then helped him tackle the baby walker he was still working on.

Picking up the instructions, she laughed. "You're right. This is almost gibberish."

"Hey, you're not done wrapping," he said.

"Oh?"

"There are still three gifts on the dining room table," he said.

She'd been in there and she thought she had wrapped everything. She rose and went into the other room and found the gifts.

"Well, someone must have just put these out there," she said.

Picking them up, she noticed three cute baby outfits and another gag gift.

"Who are these for?"

"The baby outfits are for Samantha, Emily, and Kendra," he said. "And the other as-seen-on-television gift is for you to take to the family Christmas."

Her chest tightened with excitement. It was almost too good to ask. "I'm going?"

He stopped twisting the screw in and gazed at her. "Of course, you are."

Happiness filled her and she didn't know how to act. She was not a family member, but rather an employee.

"But I'm just your nanny," she said.

"Would you stop saying that? You're more than Mia's nanny," he replied. "If I didn't bring you, the family would disown me. Besides, I want you there with me."

She smiled at him, feeling so confused. Was she just Mia's nanny? Were they working towards a relationship? What was going on? And yet when she glanced at Joshua, a fuzzy sensation filled her and the kisses they shared had left desire pulsing through her.

The man was a womanizer, but she loved how he'd taken to Mia and was learning to be a father. Learning how to take care of her, and he genuinely cared about the baby. He had a good heart but his past was what kept him from making a commitment to anyone, but she hoped Mia had changed him. Made him into the kind of man who would someday commit to a woman and a family and give him the chance at happiness.

"Thank you," she said. "Family is something I've always dreamed of having and you have such a big one. Thank you for including me."

He gave a chuckle. "Family is fun, but sometimes they can be a pain in the ass as well. Like Aunt Rose, who is so demanding. That woman thinks she's queen."

"And yet you love her and would do anything for her,"

Kayla said, knowing in her heart it was true. The woman was difficult, but at nearly eighty, she deserved to act however she wanted.

He was screwing in the wheels.

"Yes," he said. "She gave me hope when I thought all was lost. Told me that I didn't need my mother. That it was time to become a man. So I did."

She finished wrapping the gifts and sat them under the tree.

Again, she went over and picked up the instructions. "You're almost finished. She's going to love this."

"Me, a single man, putting together a baby walker on Christmas Eve," he said, laughing.

"What would you normally be doing?"

He grinned. "I'd have to kill you if I told you."

She hit him on the head with the instructions and he grabbed her arm and took her to the floor. His body was on top of hers, his groin pushing into her center. A flash of pure passion filled her and she gasped as her insides fluttered.

"Or even better, I could show you."

"And then what?"

"Darling, we'll worry about tomorrow later. Tonight I think you need me, and damn, I've needed you for weeks."

His lips covered hers and she loved the way his mouth took possession, claiming her. The slide of his tongue against her lips before he delved into her mouth, his hands pulling her tightly against him as he ground his groin into her.

With the Christmas lights twinkling, they lay on the floor and he moved her to where his hands slid down to her breasts. Just the touch of him through her clothes had her arching against him, wanting, needing him.

While she knew who he was, she also knew that on this day, she needed a man to hold her and promise her that someday her life would be what she wanted. To comfort her and help her get through this lonely season.

Tonight she needed Joshua to clear her mind of thoughts of what she'd lost a year ago and prove to her that she could move on.

She deserved a better life.

Lifting his mouth from hers, he stared down at her, the Christmas lights reflecting in his hair and eyes, reminding her that he had scars as well.

"We've been playing with fire for days now, and I need to know if this is what you want," he said to her. "You know the kind of man I am. I can't promise you that I'll change."

And that terrified her. But if she didn't agree to tonight, she would always wonder what could have been. No, she wasn't certain she could change him and wouldn't even begin to try. But, maybe, there was a chance, and if not, she'd recovered from being hurt before.

Today, she needed to feel comfort, and Joshua had done that better than anyone she'd ever met.

"No promises," she said. "Just tonight. I need you."

A grin spread across his face and he leaned down and kissed her again. His mouth was even more insistent as his hands raised her shirt and his fingers shoved aside her bra.

Ending the kiss, his mouth was on her breasts, her nipples, as he laved her areola with his tongue, sucking and nipping at her.

She groaned and her hands went to his hair as she held his head in place.

Tonight would be theirs to last them for the rest of their lives. Because as much as she had tried to guard her heart against him, she was quickly falling in love with Joshua. The man's strength of character, his love for his daughter, and the way his life revolved around his family were everything she was looking for.

Everything except his womanizing ways, which she refused to think of right now.

Rising, he quickly shed his shoes, socks, and pants until he was gloriously naked, his cock jutting proudly before him.

The urge to run her fingers over that satiny skin was almost too much.

Then he helped her undress. Finally, he slipped her silk panties from her body. Remnants of her previous business life.

When they were both naked, they lay on the carpet in front of the tree, skin against skin. Desire flooded her as she gazed into his brilliant blue eyes.

For a moment, they stared at one another and then his mouth skimmed over hers before his lips went lower.

Kayla's mind halted as she let the passion he was evoking wash over her, reveling in the sensations he created. Joshua's scent enveloped her like a tantalizing piece of chocolate and it was all she could do not to pull him up and taste him.

When his tongue swept across her breast, she arched her back in a fevered response. Heat blazed from her breasts to her belly, leaving her wanting and needy. Urgent to touch him, eager to feel him, she reached out and ran her fingertips down his face in a loving caress.

Flicking his tongue across her nipple, he moved farther down her body, his mouth trailing kisses, his tongue leaving a wet, hot trail across her heated skin. His hands reached for her knees and he spread her legs, opening her up for him.

"Beautiful," he whispered as his tongue delved between her thighs.

"Oh," she cried as she arched her back off the floor, her fingers clenching as his mouth teased her. This gorgeous, sensual man humbled himself between her legs, lovingly licking her inner folds, teasing, sending fire spiraling through her.

Unable to stop herself, she gripped the top of his head, holding his mouth against her. It had been over a year since she'd had a man give her an orgasm. Years since anyone had ever put their mouth upon her.

And so much time had passed since her heart filled full of an emotion that frightened her. Tension radiated from her center, holding her hostage until she gave into the pleasure.

"Joshua," she screamed as the orgasm gripped her and rode her like a rodeo star.

When it was over, she lay there panting, breathing hard. Joshua crawled between her legs.

Grabbing his pants, he yanked out his wallet and pulled out a condom. Thank goodness he had one because she would not let herself get pregnant again until she knew for certain they would remain together forever.

Ripping the condom package open, he quickly sheathed himself.

Once again, his fingers found the nub between her folds and slid through her center giving her pleasure. She gasped as he teased her.

"Joshua," she cried.

"What, darling?" he asked, his breathing heavy.

"Now," she cried.

"Yes," he said and plunged deep inside her.

She welcomed him as he slid within the confines of her body, gripping him inside, holding him tightly with her heart. As if he realized the impact of what they were doing, he paused and then he slowly eased almost all the way out before plunging in again.

Her need rose rapidly and she opened her eyes and stared deep into his sapphire ones, wanting to touch his soul and brand him as her own.

Unhurried, he took her mouth, his lips devouring hers. She wanted him to consume her as desire rippled through her like an aftershock. Their tongues mated and danced as his lips moved over hers.

Why with this man did she feel so much passion? Why did her body respond like it had come home?

"Joshua," she said, needing him more than anything.

With each thrust, Kayla met him halfway, her hips moving of their own accord, her body completely in tune with his. They moved as one, in unison, in perfect harmony.

Their lips broke apart and she gasped, her lungs needing more air. "Don't stop."

He smiled down at her and pounded into her again, and again, and again. Unimaginable pleasure spiraled through her, leaving her breathless and dizzy.

Magic filled her, tightening, centering, and sizzling with an intensity unlike anything she'd ever felt.

With no one else had she ever experienced such pleasure.

His blue eyes darkened as his body shuddered his release. Kayla let go of the orgasm she'd felt gathering like a storm inside her body. Tremors rippled through her as she felt her control collapsing. She clasped his back, holding him tightly, wanting to absorb him into her soul where she could cherish these moments together.

He slumped on top of her then rolled them to their sides on the carpeted floor. For a moment, the two of them lay there as their breathing returned to normal and their heartbeats slowed.

The room was silent except for the sound of their lungs heaving for more air.

Never had lovemaking been so breathtaking between her and a man. Only with Joshua.

Suddenly he stood. Reaching down he pulled her to her feet and then he lifted her into his arms.

"Next time, we're doing it in a bed," he said as he carried her down the hall.

Her heart swelled with so much emotion and she knew she was in trouble. Because she was falling in love with Joshua Burnett, the womanizer, and she feared he would break her heart, but she couldn't stop herself from loving him.

CHAPTER 20

*E*arly the next morning, Joshua and Kayla woke to the sound of Mia cooing in her crib. They went into her room and she smiled at them and kicked her legs.

"Merry Christmas, sweetie," Kayla said, grinning at the baby.

"Happy first Christmas, princess," Joshua said, knowing this one was special. And there were so many baby toys under the tree waiting for her.

"Let's change you and then you can see what Santa brought," Kayla said as the baby smiled and twitched her little legs.

While Kayla changed her, Joshua got his phone ready. He wanted pictures to remember this first Christmas.

"She's probably not going to last long before she wants her bottle," Kayla said, pulling Mia's pajamas down and snapping them between her legs. "Let's go see what Santa brought you," she said and handed the baby to Joshua.

"You take her," he said.

"No, she's your daughter and this is her first Christmas. Give me your phone and let me take a video of the two of you."

Pictures of the two of them. His heart warmed and filled with pride. His baby girl and him.

Joshua took Mia and she reached up and patted his face. He carried her into the living room.

"Look, Mia," he said. "Santa brought you presents." Something he'd never received, but he was able to give his daughter what he wanted. Because he was excited, the baby kicked her legs, smiled, and cooed at him.

When she saw the big pink giraffe standing by the tree she squealed. He took her near the giraffe and she reached out and pulled it to her. Immediately it went into her mouth.

He moved back.

"Look, your own personal baby walker," he said as he placed her in the walker.

She was still too small, and as she slipped down inside, she looked up and gave him a frown, pushing her bottom lip out.

He laughed and picked her up. "That one is for later, I guess."

He laid her beneath the tree and she raised her head to look at the lights.

"Open her presents," Kayla said.

Feeling kind of foolish, he ripped open the paper and when she saw the soft baby doll she squealed. Her little hands reached for it and he gave the doll to her. She pulled it to her mouth.

Then he opened the package that held the new dresses

SYLVIA MCDANIEL

he'd bought her. "Look, Mia, you're going to be a fashionista," he said.

She kicked her feet and giggled.

Kayla set down his phone and reached beneath the tree. "Merry Christmas, Joshua."

She'd bought him something and he quickly tore open the package. A new leather billfold and a picture of Mia in a frame.

"I thought you might want to sit it in your bedroom," she said. "And there's a small photo of her in your billfold as well."

He reached over and pulled her to him. "Thank you. I love them."

She grinned at him and kissed him on the lips. "It's not much, but a little something."

"I have something for you as well," he told her, reaching back beneath the tree to the box. He pulled it out and handed her the package.

"For you," he said.

Quickly she unwrapped the box and she gasped when she saw the new computer.

"Oh my, I needed one of these so badly and just hadn't had time to go out and get it. This is so great. Thank you," she said as she grabbed and hugged him. "It's perfect."

A rush of joy unlike anything he'd ever felt overcame him. She had tears in her eyes and he knew he'd gotten her the perfect gift.

"Yours was pretty out of date," he said.

"Yes, and I can use this new one for the business," she said, ripping into the box and reading all the information.

"The man at the store said it was the latest model," he told her. Never before had he given a gift that someone was so happy to receive.

She looked up at him and smiled. "This is the best Christmas gift I've ever received. Thank you again."

The happiness on her face left him feeling so much joy. He liked seeing Kayla smile and making her elated.

A few minutes later Mia began to cry. "Time to fix her breakfast. When do we need to be at the clubhouse?"

"Noon," he said. "The family gathers for a Christmas prayer and lunch and then we have the exchange."

A smile spread across Kayla's face. "Thank you for inviting me."

"Come on, let's get ready," he said.

Several hours later, they walked into the clubhouse, and Kayla took the dish they had prepared to the kitchen. Mia wore a sparkly Christmas dress and his daughter was oohed and aahed over by the entire family.

A fierce feeling of papa pride overcame him as the women fawned over the baby.

With his family all gathered, he couldn't imagine spending Christmas any other way. A big Christmas tree stood in the corner decorated with presents beneath. For as long as he could remember, they had gathered on this day. And every year during his childhood, his parents argued over attending. His mother thought the Burnetts were crude which was probably the reason he fit in so much better with his father's side of the family.

He couldn't even remember the last time he'd been to a gathering of his mother's family. He and his brothers had never been invited once his mother passed away. And that was fine. They were snobs and the atmosphere had always been stuffy.

Here, everyone, for the most part, got along and there was always lots of food, fun, and laughter.

Jacob and Justin, his two brothers, sidled up to him. "Merry Christmas, brother."

"Merry Christmas to you."

"Where is our niece? We want to spoil her a little," Jacob said.

"Are you going to keep her?" Justin asked, his blue eyes worried.

"Haven't made that decision yet," he said.

After last night, he was more confused than ever. Maybe sleeping with Mia's nanny had not been the best idea he'd had. But it had been wonderful, and the sex more fulfilling than he could remember.

But Kayla was not a woman to agree to a fling or a one-night stand and marriage scared the living hell out of him. He'd seen the worst of the institution, and he just didn't know if he could ever marry anyone.

"What's holding you back?" Justin said. "She's your daughter. She should be with you."

That was true. But was he a capable, good parent who would give her the love and attention she needed? He had to do what was best for Mia.

"Being a parent, you have to put your children's well-being before your own. I'm trying to make the right decision."

"That's easy," Jacob said. "She needs to stay here. We know what it's like to be raised by a mother more interested in entertaining and society than her children. And Mia's grandparents are right up there with our mother."

That was the problem. He wasn't certain about them. Skylar told him she was raised by nannies, but he wanted to speak to her parents before he made his decision. He missed his old life. The carefree going out and partying till dawn and sleeping until noon. He missed dancing the night away. And women.

Just then Kayla walked through the room with Mia in her stroller. She must have had to change the infant because she had disappeared.

Staring at her, he wanted to grab her hand and take her back to his house and spend the rest of the day in bed, exploring her body.

The woman was beautiful. She was kind and sweet and had a strong backbone that life had not been able to break. She was tough.

And last night had conjured up feelings he couldn't ever remember feeling about a woman.

"Are you still with us," Jacob asked. His eyes widened. "Oh, no, you slept with the nanny. Dear God, is nothing sacred to you?"

Joshua turned and glared at his brothers. "What are you talking about?"

"That look in your eyes," Justin said. "I've been around you at the clubs. I know how you like to pursue a woman, bed her, and walk away. You've got that look in your eyes."

Even his brothers thought of him as a hound-dogging womanizer. And he was...could he change? Could he be a one-woman kind of man?

Especially when he missed going out to the bars.

"If I'm sleeping with the nanny, that is none of your business. As for being a womanizer, people can and often do change."

His brothers started laughing.

"Yes, and our mother was a nun," Jacob said. "I think I need to warn Kayla. She's too sweet for you to rip her heart to shreds. Did you ever think that your actions are just like our mother's?"

Joshua jerked his head toward his brother Jacob, his fists clenched ready to swing at the man. And then like a load of horse manure, it hit him.

His mother was a whore. She cheated on their father. Even after they divorced, she was often at the country club looking for a man right up until she came down with breast cancer.

Just like Joshua—a man-whore. While he said he was doing it to keep from growing close to a woman, what if his mother had done it to keep from growing close to a man?

Even Kayla had mentioned that maybe he was acting like his mother. But until now, he never really considered that it was his way of keeping women away from him. Just like his mother did his father.

"It's Christmas," he said, taking a deep breath. "Today is not the day for us to air out our dirty laundry for everyone to see. And right now, I'm about ready to punch you, Jacob, so I suggest you take your comparing me to our mother to the other side of the room."

His brother had studied psychology in college, and oftentimes, he tried to help others see their issues. And right now,

Joshua didn't want to see that he was in any way acting like his mother.

His brothers walked away and he stood there staring at Kayla and Mia, wishing he was different. Wishing he was the kind of man who could be what Kayla needed. What Mia needed.

But if he was like his mother, then he would never inflict himself on anyone permanently.

His Aunt Rose walked up to him.

"That daughter of yours is beautiful," she said. "I can't wait to see you fighting the boys off her."

What could he say? He'd been run out of the yard by a couple of daddies who were protecting their daughters when he was much younger.

"Thanks for the jacket. I love western leather coats and mine was just about worn out," she said. "You're awfully quiet today."

He turned and glanced at her. "My brothers just said I act like my mother. Is that true?"

A grin spread across Aunt Rose's face. "You know, when I met your mother, I really liked her. She was so in love with your father and then after Jacob was born, she changed. I don't know what happened. People change. And she started pursuing men. Your father was devastated, but he kept trying to make the marriage work until one day she walked in and said she wanted a divorce."

He knew all this, but it was good to hear it from someone who had been an adult at that time.

"Are you like her? No," she said. "But you're so determined

not to let a woman close to you that you often make wrong choices."

She glanced at Kayla. "Now, that girl there is the type of woman who won't let anyone take advantage of her. I think life has toughened her. So don't think about cheating on her unless you want her to walk away. Because she would."

He cocked his head and stared at his aunt. "How do you know Kayla is that tough?"

"I did a background check on her. No one was going to take care of my great-niece without me knowing she was all right. Kayla seems like a good soul who fate has not treated fairly. Did you know in college, she was often times homeless until she could get back into the dorms?"

"No," he said, remembering how she told him she had stayed with friends.

"And she's done well for herself since she got out of college until she got mixed up with that David Frantz. That family is high society trash. She's better off without that loser."

Gazing out at Kayla, he sighed.

Aunt Rose continued. "I'd marry that girl, if I were you. She's a keeper. Oh, and I think you owe me a hog pen cleaning," his aunt said and then she moved on.

Damn, how did she know?

Marry her? The words sent fear spiraling through him. Could he give up his single life and marry Kayla?

If he was going to marry anyone, it would be her. There was so much about her that he enjoyed. She made him a better man. And he loved the way he could see excitement and the possibilities shining from her eyes when she spoke of her company.

Tucker walked up to him and grinned. "Your daughter is precious. We can't wait to see our baby."

The whole expecting part Joshua had missed out on and that made him feel sad. He would've liked to have seen Skylar's belly expanding and then he realized, no he wouldn't. She was the wrong woman.

But if it was Kayla, he would be so excited and that thought frightened him. What in the hell was wrong with him? In the three weeks that Mia had been in his life, had he completely changed?

"Just wait until you get to change the stinky diapers. That's the challenge of being a parent."

Laughter came from Tucker and he stared at him. "You change her diapers?"

"Yes, sometimes," he said. "Kayla likes to give us time together and so the evenings are mine to spend with the baby."

Shaking his head, the man reached out and patted him on the back. "Good," he said. "You've changed so much from the wild, crazy single man who chased just about any skirt. I'm glad."

The man walked away and Joshua stood there staring at Kayla talking to Samantha who was holding Mia.

His heart filled with an emotion he didn't recognize. A feeling of being protective and wanting to give her the world came over him.

What did love feel like? Was he falling in love with her?

$\mathcal{K}$ayla had never experienced a family Christmas like this one. Sitting next to Joshua when they called her number, she went up and choose a package under the tree.

Grinning, she stood and unwrapped it. It was a bug zapper in the shape of a badminton racket

"Thank you," she said. "I'm sure I can sit on the deck and swat flies with this."

She sat and Joshua grinned at her.

Tucker stood. "I'm going to steal that bug zapper from you."

"Hey, I wanted to keep this," she said.

"Welcome to the Burnett Family Christmas where everything is up for grabs up to the last gift."

She stood and looked around the room and saw that Emily had what she wanted. "I'll take the wine opener."

"You wouldn't take from a pregnant woman, would you?"

"Yes, I would. I'm the nanny and I *need* the wine opener," she said.

For the next hour, they went back and forth, the entire family playing. Desiree stole the wine opener from her and she had to take candles from Kendra.

When they finally reached the end, she gazed at Joshua. "That was so much fun."

"It can get crazy," he said and lifted a very sleepy baby from his lap. "I think it's time we took this little munchkin home and put her to bed."

"Agree," she said.

She got the stroller and he put Mia in.

Samantha came up and gave her a hug, her big belly getting in the way. "I'm so glad you joined us today. Merry Christmas."

"Thank you," Kayla said. "It was fun. You're so very blessed to be part of a large family."

"Joshua, behave yourself," she told him as she turned and walked away.

Aunt Rose came over to her. "Kayla, how is Joshua treating you?"

"Good," she replied. "And I'm so glad I got to spend Christmas with your family. Thank you."

His aunt raised her brows and looked at Joshua.

"We're glad you were here. And Mia looks healthy and happy."

"Merry Christmas," Kayla said.

As they walked out the door, Joshua shook his head. "You just got Aunt Rose's blessing and you don't even know it."

"Why would I need her blessing?" she asked.

"Nothing goes on at the Burnett Ranch that my aunt doesn't know about," he said. "If you think Eugenia is bad, Aunt Rose is worse. Far worse."

She laughed. "I think you're a little prejudiced."

"Oh no, she took me to task many times when I was growing up. But she also helped me when life became unbearable in our house," he said. "I owe her a lot."

He rolled the stroller down the lane with a sleeping Mia still in her Christmas finery.

All day, Kayla had put aside thoughts of what she and Joshua had done last night. It had been a wonderful, magical night that, while she loved what was happening between them, she knew better than to get her hopes up that it meant anything.

He was not a man who made promises.

And she was not a woman he could use anytime he wanted. She needed a commitment and she didn't think he was capable.

But for now, she would accept what he gave her and try not to make it anything more than what it was.

But spending today with the Burnetts had been a fairy tale for a woman like her. Her Christmas memories were made up of different families giving her a little slice of their family life while she was with them, but nothing like the Burnetts.

"When we get home, I'm going to bathe Mia, feed her, and put her to bed. She's had a long, exciting day."

The sun had sunk and a chilly breeze blew as they hurried toward his house.

"I feel like a Christmas movie tonight," he said. "How about you?"

"What's your favorite?"

"*Die Hard*," he said, laughing.

"Oh, good grief. Mine is *It's a Wonderful Life*," she said.

They had reached the house and he carried the stroller up.

"I'll fix us a snack and get the movies ready while you put Mia to bed."

"I like that idea," she said.

Mia woke as they carried her inside. She picked up the child and took her to the bathroom where her bathtub lay. While she was taking care of her, she could see the child's eyes kept closing. The baby was tired and would go down quickly.

How did they go from last night to watching movies together? What happened next or was last night just a one-time moment of weakness?

All she knew was that she could feel herself falling in love with Joshua and while she was doing her best not to get excited, she wanted more than anything to be a part of his life. For the two of them to make a family with Mia and eventually even have more children.

But she couldn't think of that right now. It was too early and he could revert to his wild ways at any moment.

Just as she lifted Mia from the tub, she heard the doorbell ring.

"Surprise," she heard a female say, giggling.

Lifting the baby to her shoulder, she walked through the house to the other side where her room and Mia's room were right next to each other. As she passed through the house, she saw a woman in a Christmas nightie that showed just about all of her, standing just inside the door.

"Marcy, this is not a good time," he told her.

He didn't tell the woman to leave and never return, he just told her not now. Picking up the coat she had dropped, he wrapped it around her and walked her out the door.

Like a dash of cold water, Kayla realized he was still the same man.

Laying Mia in her bed, she quickly put her pajamas on her and then picked up the bottle she had left warming.

Sitting in the chair, she rocked the baby and wondered how she was going to stay here if he decided to continue his ways of going to the bar and finding a different woman each night. She could not put up with that kind of behavior. Ever.

Looking down at the baby who was gazing at her with sleepy eyes, she knew it would rip her heart into shreds if she had to leave, but Mia wasn't hers.

No matter what she wanted, this baby was Joshua's, and at any time, he could end her employment. And she had foolishly let herself get involved with her employer again.

When was she going to learn not to get emotionally involved? Again, she had let herself be vulnerable and now she would once again suffer all because she'd let her guard down.

And yet at this moment, she was falling in love with Joshua. So how did she handle this situation? Right now, she just couldn't leave Mia.

The baby's lips stop sucking, her eyes were closed and she leaned her against her shoulder and she gave a little burp before she snuggled back down to sleep.

"Merry Christmas, Mia," she said softly as she laid her in her bed and tucked the covers up around her. "I'm sorry your mother is missing watching you grow."

Picking up the baby monitor, she walked out the door and closed it softly behind her.

When she went into the living room, a fire was blazing in the hearth, the Christmas lights were on and Joshua paced the floor.

"Let me explain," he said.

That surprised her.

"Marcy came over here without calling to ask me. She was going to surprise me. She thought I had gotten rid of the baby and she was ready to start things back up. But she's gone forever. After I got her outside, I told her that we were through. I'm not certain what's going on between us, but we don't need another woman interfering."

A smile spread across her face. "Thank you. I was going to tell you if that's what you want, that's fine, but I'm done."

"No, that's not what I want. What I want is right here in front of me," he said, moving toward her. "I'm still not certain about the future, but I'm willing to explore things between us. You're sexy as hell, and damn, Kayla, I like you. Give me time to decide."

Hope flooded her. What he was asking seemed reasonable, and she liked the fact that he had sent Marcy out the door, never to return.

"Time, I can give you. But I will not share my time with any other woman, do you understand?"

"Yes," he said. "Just like I won't share my time with another man."

She grinned. "Good to know."

He pulled her to him and covered her mouth with his, his tongue skimming along her lower lip.

SYLVIA MCDANIEL

When they broke apart, he sighed. "We better get started watching movies or we'll run out of time."

"We've got all night," she said softly.

A groan escaped from him.

"I knew I should have put a television in my bedroom," he said.

She giggled. "And we would not have watched the movies."

"You're right," he said.

CHAPTER 22

*J*oshua awoke to the sound of a baby crying. Squinting, he slowly opened his eyes and realized it was still dark. Reaching out beside him, he felt the bed was cold. Kayla was gone.

So why was Mia still crying if Kayla was not in bed with him?

Rising, he pulled on a pair of soft lounge pants and walked toward the other side of the house to find out what was going on. Why was Mia crying insistently in the middle of the night?

That wasn't like the baby. She had slept through the night almost from the time Kayla arrived.

When he reached the nursery, Kayla was rocking Mia who lay against her chest her face red, her nose running.

"What's wrong?"

"I don't know," she said. "She won't stop crying and she feels warm."

He laid his hand against her forehead and could feel that she was running a temperature.

"Do we have a thermometer?"

"No, that was one item, I forgot to buy," Kayla said her eyes glassy with worry. "I've given her some baby aspirin, but she won't stop crying, and so far, her fever hasn't gone down. I've done everything I know to do," she said.

He took the baby from her and Mia laid her head on his chest and cried. He walked the floor, knowing she liked that, but still she cried.

Snot ran from her nose onto his chest, but he didn't care. He didn't like seeing her this way. Mia was a happy baby unless she needed a change or she was hungry. And it looked like Kayla had tried both. A full bottle sat next to the rocker and he could feel that Mia was not wet.

Occasionally, her fingers would reach up and tug at her ear.

Five minutes later, he shook his head.

"We've got to find out why she's crying. Time to go to the emergency room," he said. "She's got a fever, somethings wrong and we're not going to wait until morning."

Kayla sighed and stood. "Good. You hold her while I get dressed and then you can change."

Within ten minutes, they were dressed and running out the door. Kayla put her in the car seat and sat in the back seat beside Mia. It was all Joshua could do not to race to the hospital. There were deer on the back roads, and it would do them no good to hit one and not be able to reach their destination.

Even though there was no traffic, it seemed to take forever to reach the local hospital.

When they arrived, Kayla jumped out of the truck and carried Mia inside.

"Park the truck and come in," she said.

He hurried as quickly as he could. When he walked in the door, he heard the nurse asking Kayla questions.

"Are you the mother?"

"No, she's dead. Mia is in the custody of her father, who is parking the car," she told the nosy nurse.

"I'm here," he said loudly.

"When did this start?"

Joshua had to take a deep breath. Why were all these questions necessary? Just find out what was wrong with the baby. She would stop crying and then a few minutes later whimper and begin to cry again.

Kayla answered the questions while he sat there fuming. What had he done to make her sick? Was it the Christmas tree? Being around his family? Or maybe even when they walked her home in the cool night air last night.

Whatever it was he would never do it again. He'd give his right arm to make her feel better.

This was why he didn't need to be responsible for her. What if he somehow killed her because of his stupidity in taking care of babies? He never meant to be a father.

Filled with anguish, he watched his baby girl curl up in Kayla's lap.

"I'm going to take you back to a room. The doctor will be with you shortly," the nurse said. "There's a lot of respiratory infections going around. Let's hope she doesn't have RSV. Many babies have to be hospitalized if they come down with that."

The nurse walked out the door and Joshua just about exploded. "RSV? What the hell? Where would she have caught that? Hospitalizing her?" He ran his hands through his hair. "I can't stand seeing her in pain. What did we do wrong?"

Inside the small exam room, he paced, more anxious than he'd ever felt in his life.

"Joshua, babies get sick. Kids get sick. Their immune systems are weak when they're born, and by getting sick, they get stronger."

"No," he said. "I'm a terrible father. I almost starved her to death. I nearly dropped her on her head. And now this."

Sitting in a chair in the exam room, Kayla comforted Mia who was in her arms. "It's okay, baby. Daddy is just worried about you."

He glanced around at all the instruments in the room and wondered how many kids had come in here. Hell, he didn't even know if she'd had all her shots that babies need. What if Skylar had missed one, and now she was sick because he put that off until her grandparents returned?

"We should have taken her to a pediatrician when she first arrived," he said.

"I was waiting until you made your final decision before I suggested that," Kayla said.

He whirled around to face her. "But what if she missed a dose of something and now, she has typhoid or meningitis or polo or something horrible? What if she dies because of me?"

Kayla didn't say anything for a few minutes but watched him. "You're acting like a father who cares for his daughter and is worried about her."

"Of course, I am," he said.

Just then the doctor walked in the door.

"Hello," she said. "I'm Doctor Ann Peters. What's going on with the little one."

"She's sick," Joshua said, knowing he was being unreasonable, but unable to stop himself.

"Well, let's take a look at her," the doctor said with a smile.

"She woke me up at three a.m. crying. Normally, she sleeps through the night," Kayla said. "She's running a fever and baby aspirin didn't seem to bring it down."

The doctor opened Mia's pajamas and listened to her chest. "She's a little congested."

"Were you around a lot of people yesterday?"

"Yes," Joshua said. "And some idiot must have made her sick."

"Is this your firstborn," the doctor asked.

"Yes," Joshua said.

"The first ones are always the ones you worry about the most," the doctor replied. "Let's look in her ears."

It was all Joshua could do not to throttle the doctor. She was a paid professional, shouldn't she know what was wrong with her?

"Ah, here's the problem," the doctor said. "She has an ear infection. Poor baby's ears are red, swollen, and pressing against her ear drums. She's in pain."

It was an ear infection, really?

The doctor looked up her nose. "I'm not seeing a sinus infection. I think we caught it before it spread. I'm going to give you some antibiotics and ear drops. I suggest you get a vaporizer to put in her room. That will help her breathe. We don't want this going any further than her ears. Keep her at home, and in three days if she's not better, I would recommend you take her to your pediatrician."

Joshua ran his hand through his hair. A damn ear infection? He thought they had killed her and she was dying from something they did to her.

"She's going to be fine," the doctor said, gazing at him. "She's a healthy, beautiful baby and you're taking great care of her. But babies get sick."

His legs were shaking and he plopped into a chair. "I thought we'd done something to her."

The doctor laughed. "You have. You're raising a baby and sometimes that can be stressful."

He didn't need this kind of stress.

He loved Mia. He wanted her to grow up to be a beautiful young woman but he wasn't certain he could raise her. Not if he feared hurting her. What if they'd done something that couldn't be reversed?

"All right, folks. You can get this prescription filled at a local pharmacy. Don't take her out in the cold if you can help it and always make certain her ears are covered."

"We didn't cover her ears last night," Joshua said.

"No, we didn't," Kayla said.

"Live and learn," the doctor said. "She's going to be fine."

"But will I?" Joshua mumbled.

The doctor laughed. "You're a worried father. Good night, folks. Try to get some rest. Mia is going to be fine."

As they walked out the door, Mia snuggled up against Joshua who had picked her up. What was he doing? He could be at the club dancing the night away, picking up women, and instead he was at the emergency room, taking care of his daughter.

All because he'd not thought to cover her ears when they walked home last night. What kind of father did that to his child?

CHAPTER 23

*W*hen they arrived home, Joshua was unable to go back to sleep. It was almost five in the morning and Kayla had put warm drops in the baby's ear and given her the antibiotic.

She fell asleep with Kayla rocking her.

Joshua on the other hand paced the floor.

It was only an ear infection, but it could have been something so much worse. What was he doing?

Skylar's parents were due in anytime. They had raised a child before, even though they had not done a good job, they could at least hire people to take good care of her. Better care than Joshua.

What if they had not taken her to the emergency room? The infection could have gotten worse. It could have turned into RSV. He was a lousy father.

Gazing in the room, Kayla had fallen asleep with the baby on her shoulder. Just gazing at the two of them, pain gripped his chest. His feelings for Kayla had grown so much in the last week that he was afraid. Frightened beyond belief, and even Mia, he wanted the best for her and he wasn't certain he could provide what she needed.

It was time to let her return to her grandparents. Oh, how he wished Skylar had not been killed, but hopefully her parents would love and care for Mia the way she needed.

Sinking onto the couch, he leaned forward and put his head in his hands. No one ever said that making the right decision for a child was easy. And he only hoped and prayed that he was making the best choice for his daughter.

She deserved a good life, the very best life had to offer, and he just wasn't certain he could give her the attention she needed. Soon she would be crawling, then walking and talking, and if he kept her, it would be a lifetime commitment.

If he let her grandparents raise her, he could see her whenever he chose.

How would Kayla handle his decision?

Hopefully, she would understand. And he would really like for her to stay with him during this difficult time of letting the baby go. They could comfort each other knowing that he had made the best decision for Mia.

At eight o'clock, he received a message from the guards that he had a visitor. A Mr. and Mrs. Beal. Time to meet them and let them know he had decided to let them raise Mia.

He went into the nursery and woke Kayla.

"Her grandparents are here," he told her.

"Oh," she said and stood to change Mia.

The baby was groggy and he could tell she still didn't feel good. Was it fair to send her with them when she was ill?

Inside his chest, his heart warred with his head, and yet he refused to back down from his decision. He was doing what was best for the baby.

A car pulled up in front of the house and he glanced out the window. It was a big black stretch limo.

Obviously, they had the money to give Mia the best. When they knocked on the door, he answered.

"Kenneth Beal," the man said, offering his hand. "And this is my wife Claire."

"Hello," the woman said.

"Please come in and sit," he said. "I'm so sorry about Skylar."

They both nodded as they sat on his couch, the father in his very expensive suit and Skylar's mother dressed in a designer pantsuit that he was certain she wouldn't want baby puke on.

"The police report says she was drunk. I'm not surprised," her father said.

Her mother blinked back tears. "How is Mia?"

"Well, we had to take her to the ER this morning. She has an ear infection. She's not feeling very good."

"Poor motherless baby," Claire said. "While I love my grandchild. I'm so busy that it's going to be hard to take care of her."

Just then Kayla walked in with Mia. She was wearing one of the new dresses that Joshua had bought her and she looked so stinking cute, he wasn't certain he could let her go. But he had to, for her sake.

"This is Kayla Scott, the nanny I hired," he told them.

"Hello," she said, smiling.

They nodded, but really didn't acknowledge her.

"As her father, you have the legal rights to her," Kenneth Beal said.

This was his chance to back out of his previous decision and tell them he had decided to keep her. But he wanted the best for his daughter and last night had frightened him. The thought of doing something to her that harmed her scared him.

"I've thought long and hard about this," he said, wanting to change his mind, but his head refused to let him. "For me, it's all about who has her best interest at heart. After last night, I think she would be safer with you than with me."

A loud gasp came from Kayla. "Are you crazy?"

He turned and gazed at her, seeing the pain on her face. "Babies get sick. We did what was right. We took her to the doctor. She'll be fine in a few days."

Anger tightened his chest. She was doubting his decision. Hell, he was doubting his decision, but it had to be the best for Mia.

"I'm doing what I think is best for my daughter," he said, trying to put her in her place.

Kayla shook her head in disbelief. "I thought you had changed. But you aren't doing what's best for Mia, you're doing what's best for you. This is so you can go out and live your happy, free, single life again. So you can create another child and walk away from her."

Now that was out of line.

"No, that's not true at all. Because of our parental stupidity, we didn't cover her ears and she got sick. What other stupid things are we going to do that will harm her? Next time, we could kill her and then I'd be devastated. This way, she has grandparents who raised children before and know how to take care of them."

"All parents make mistakes. But good parents don't walk away from their children, even after they make a mistake," she said her eyes filling with tears. "I'll go get her ready."

Kayla turned and walked away.

Joshua turned back to the Beals and they stared at him.

"We'll hire a good nanny," Mrs. Beal said. "Someone who knows her place."

He had to defend Kayla. "She's a great nanny. She's taken good care of Mia and didn't let me do things that would not have been good for her. Kayla is just upset that I'm giving her to you."

Kenneth shook his head. "Our daughter should never have gotten pregnant or at least had an abortion. And believe me, we tried to talk her into not having Mia or even giving her up for adoption. We want to spend the rest of our lives traveling and don't have time to care for our grand-daughter."

Warning sirens blared in his brain and yet he still believed they could take better care of her than he could. This morning had shaken him and he wanted Mia to grow into a beautiful woman.

Kayla stepped out of the nursery and shoved Mia into his arms. She set the diaper bag at his feet. "She's ready."

Then she turned and walked away. Holding his daughter, his heart shattered inside his chest.

"I will want to see her occasionally," he said. Right now, he couldn't commit to a schedule.

"Of course," Claire said. "But call us in advance. We may

not be available and after I hire the right nanny, they will be told not to let strangers have her."

Damn, was he making the right choice?

He held her close and she gazed up at him. Her little hand reached up and touched his cheek.

God, was he doing the right thing? He wanted her to have the best life possible.

With a sigh, he handed the baby to Claire.

"Mia," she said softly.

The baby's face puckered up in a frown and she begin to cry.

"She has an ear infection. The doctor sent home ear drops and antibiotics and said if she wasn't better in three days to take her to her pediatrician."

"We'll take good care of her," Kenneth told Joshua.

A commotion came from the hall and Kayla walked into the room with her suitcase.

"Where are you going?"

"I'm leaving. You have no need for my services," she said. "Best of luck. Hope you find your Santa at the bar tonight."

Joshua didn't know what to say. She wasn't even going to give them a chance. She was walking out the door.

"Can't we talk," he said.

"Nothing to talk about. You chose your single life over me and Mia. Enjoy."

Damn it, no he hadn't. He wanted what was best for Mia. Kayla picked up her suitcase and walked out the door, leaving him with the Beals.

"I'd file a complaint with the agency she's working for," Mrs. Beal said as she rose. "Kenneth, it's time to get home.

There are lots of things to do and we have to start interviewing nannies for Mia."

"Good luck," Mr. Beal said as they stood and walked out the door. He picked up the diaper bag and they hurried to their limo.

As Joshua closed the door, the silence in the house seemed to close in on him. He was alone. Totally and utterly alone for the first time in three weeks. And the silence was suffocating.

What had he just done?

As he sank down on the couch, the smell of lavender overwhelmed him.

"I've never been more disappointed in one of my grandsons than I am right now. Even my son didn't disappoint me this badly. You gave away your daughter."

"I'm trying to give her the best possible life," he said.

"With those people? What are you seeing that I don't? They don't give two hoots and a holler about that child. They are too busy traveling to give Mia the love and attention she needs."

Maybe Eugenia was right, but he'd made his decision.

"Because we didn't cover her ears, she got sick," he said. "I'm not a good father. I'll never be a good husband, and frankly, right now, I hate my life."

The ghost shimmered in front of him and he could see she was furious with him. "She got sick because she's a baby. There will be many more illnesses and hopefully she'll recover from them. You're a great father and just don't realize it. And as for being a good husband, if you would only allow yourself to feel your emotions, you would be a wonderful husband for Kayla.

"As for hating your life. That's because you've made some really bad choices. So now go out to the bars tonight and find yourself a woman who will let you have sex with her. That should just seal your horrible life. Lose yourself at the bar and forget your misery."

Damn, he was calling a ghost hunter and getting her out of here.

"All right, I will," he said, thinking that was what he needed. A good evening of dancing and drinking and bringing someone home to dull the memories of Kayla in his bed. To wipe the pain his heart was feeling from his mind.

"I'm going to haunt you until you bring her back," Eugenia promised him.

"And I'm calling a ghost hunter to remove you," he said.

"Challenge accepted. As I said before, I'll have him running out of this house frightened beyond his wildest dreams."

With a swirl, the ghost disappeared.

Later that evening, he sat in the bar and glanced around. The band was deafening and he wondered if that was so people were not inclined to talk. Same people. Same women. Same cowboys looking to hook up.

"Hey, there," a woman he couldn't even remember her name said to him as he sat nursing his beer.

"Hello," he said.

"Wanna dance," she asked.

"Sure," he replied. He had to start participating and not just sitting at the bar wishing he was somewhere else.

The woman pressed into him and they begin to dance.

"Haven't seen you in a while."

"Been taking care of some business," he said, the smell of

Mia smacking him in the face. That sweet baby smell, not the one when she pooped in her diaper. The sound of her laugh when she was happy echoed in his head. How she would blow bubbles and coo.

And Kayla, always there taking care of her, laughing and playing with her. One side of her was the good mother and the other side of Kayla was a sexual goddess. Taking him to heights of pleasure he had never experienced.

Why was sex so perfect with her? Why did she push him to be a better man, a good father, and even an improved person? And yet here he was in the bar trying to return to his old life.

What was he doing? Had he lost his mind? Sure, he'd make mistakes as a father, but right now, the biggest mistake he'd made was giving his daughter to those people. Skylar had cautioned him about her parents and he'd pushed aside her warning, thinking they would take care of his daughter.

And no, they were not right for her. She needed him and Kayla.

"Excuse me," he said, stepping away from the woman on the dance floor. "I've been really stupid and I need to make things right. Enjoy your evening."

Walking out of the club, he went to his truck and looked up Skylar's parents' address. He was going to get Mia back, right now. And then he was going to find Kayla. That was going to be the biggest challenge. What hotel was she staying in now?

And then he was going to have to do some really strong apologizing because he had majorly screwed up.

CHAPTER 24

ayla glanced around the weekly hotel rental apartment she sat in. The walls were a drab brown and she wondered if that was to hide the wear these units received. In one corner was a small kitchenette with a refrigerator and microwave. On the other side sat a television, loveseat, and chair.

Small, quaint, and affordable.

Another hotel, another job lost, another stupid move of falling for her boss. When would she learn not to care too much for the most powerful man in her life?

When would she give up on finding the family of her dreams and just accepting that she would always be alone? Why did she fall for men who were not for her?

After spending three weeks with Joshua, she knew he was a good man. A better man than the life he led. During that time, he had not gone out to the bar once. Every evening, he came in from working the cattle and he'd spent the evenings with Mia.

After she went to bed, they spent time talking and getting to know one another. It had been a fun time that she convinced herself could become something more.

She really believed he had changed and he loved Mia. But a little ear infection had sent him running back to his old life. And if he couldn't take the thought of Mia getting sick, then maybe he wasn't meant to be her father.

Babies got sick and hopefully they got to the doctor quickly enough to get them the medication they needed. Children fell and scuffed their knees and elbows and sometimes even broke a bone.

They were kids learning about life, and sometimes they experienced pain. And as a parent, you went through it with them.

And Mia. Her chest ached with anguish at the loss of that sweet child. No, she wasn't hers, but still she fell in love with that baby like she was her own. It nearly killed her to leave her while she was sick. And even now, she wondered how she was doing.

She was certain Mr. and Mrs. Beal would never take her call if she wanted to find out about her. Those people were cold.

The memory of Joshua telling them they should take Mia caused her stomach to cramp. Just thinking about him, her eyes filled with tears.

He was a better person than how he'd acted. She'd been utterly shocked at him giving Mia to Skylar's parents. And she couldn't help but wonder how his family had reacted to the news.

She was certain Eugenia would probably haunt him for

days if not weeks, but what about Aunt Rose? His cousins? Even his own brothers? How would they all accept the news that he had given up Mia?

Deep down, she truly believed he loved the child but was terrified of hurting Mia. Terrified of giving her the life his parents had given him. And yet, Skylar's parents reminded her of the way he described his own parents.

If only he would look in the mirror and realize he was acting just as bad as his mother had when she divorced his father. But she would never be the one to tell him this. He had to make that realization on his own.

Though he tried to keep walls up around him so as not to act like his mother, he'd done exactly what he feared.

And the look on his face when she walked out with her suitcase in hand didn't surprise her. He couldn't believe she was leaving him, but there was no reason to stay because she would never accept the way the old Joshua behaved, and it seemed he'd returned to the way he was before Mia.

As much as she loved him, she would not be a part of his wild, partying ways.

With a sigh, she lay on the bed and stared up at the ceiling, seeing a water stain. Maybe her time as a nanny was over. After Mia, she couldn't think of giving up another child. She couldn't put her heart and soul into taking care of a baby only to walk out when they no longer needed her.

Maybe it was time she got her business going and made it on her own. No more bosses. No more babies until she could have her own. And maybe she didn't need a husband to have her own child.

Time to strike out on her own.

Rising from the bed, she wiped the tears from her eyes and sat at the computer she'd brought with her. The computer that Joshua had purchased for her. Time for her to put all thoughts of him and Mia behind her.

What she needed to do now was bury herself in her work. Focus on getting her company going. Then she could show them all that this little foster girl could make it on her own without a husband or a family behind her.

The strength resided in her because she had overcome so many odds to get to where she was. Only now, she needed to dig a little deeper and overcome this latest setback.

For the next hour, she sent out emails to her previous clients. She asked if they would give her a phone interview and let her talk about how she could help them grow their business with the tailored marketing plan she could create for them.

Immediately she had five responses asking her where she was working, what was she doing, and yes, please they wanted to speak to her.

An hour later, she stood and stretched. It was time to fix Mia's dinner. Her heart clenched. And, damn, it was time for Joshua to come home. But that life was gone and a sob escaped from her.

The people next door started to play loud music, their boom box shaking the walls. What had she done to deserve this? No matter who she tried to give her love to, it seemed they always disappointed and hurt her. And now she was back living in a hotel, trying to make a living.

Sinking down on the bed, she sobbed, her heart breaking,

cursing Joshua in her mind. She had done nothing wrong but fall in love with her boss.

She deserved better.

CHAPTER 25

On his way to the Beals', he fully realized the consequence of his actions. Claire reminded him of his mother and he had just resigned Mia to a life like his own childhood.

What the hell was wrong with him? Why had he not seen the warning signs before now?

Yes, he was going back for her, but until this moment, he hadn't seen how Skylar's parents were just like his mother. No, he'd not had nannies growing up, but that was because of his father. If his mother had her way, she would've had nothing to do with her children.

Claire didn't seem overly eager to spend time with Mia. He had to get his daughter back.

When he pulled up in front of their spacious mansion, he parked his truck and walked up the sidewalk.

Ringing the bell, the housekeeper came to the door. He could hear Mia in the background screaming. That couldn't be good for her ear infection. What if she suffered permanent damage because of his stupidity?

He was going to make mistakes as a father. But once he recognized he was wrong, he would need to make an immediate correction. And that was what he was here doing.

"I've come for her," he said and pushed past the housekeeper. "Where is she?"

The maid grinned. "Up the stairs, second door on the right. They're ignoring her because they think she'll stop crying."

Dear God, that was how the parented?

"Tell them I'm here and that I've come to get her," he said, taking the stairs two at a time.

When he opened the door, she was lying there, her bottom lip trembling, her chest shaking with sobs. He was her worst enemy, but he promised that he would not fail her again.

"I'm sorry, princess. Sometimes your daddy makes horrible decisions and this was one. It's time to take you home," he said.

She gave a little hiccup but stopped crying. A smile crept over her face and she kicked her legs.

"We've got to wrap you up tight and cover those ears. We don't want you getting any sicker," he said.

Grabbing her diaper bag, he realized they had not even unpacked it. They were waiting for the nanny to unpack her.

"We're going home," he said.

"Joshua, what are you doing?" Claire Beal said as she stood at the door.

"I've come to take my daughter home. I've changed my mind," he said.

The woman sighed. "Are you sure this is a good idea?"

"I'm certain of it," he said. "You don't want her."

The woman didn't disagree. "I've had my children. She's Skylar's daughter."

"Who is dead. Did you even mourn her?"

"How dare you," she said. "Of course, I did. We had a small memorial service for her on the boat."

At least they did that.

"Good," he said. "I'd like to have a picture of Skylar so Mia knows what her mother looked like. I want her to know a little about her."

The woman sighed and then she turned to the maid. "Take that picture of Skylar off the wall in the family room. He can have that one."

Kenneth was waiting for him at the bottom of the stairs as he made his way down.

"We're too old for babies," he said. "I'm glad you came back for her. She's been a trial."

He couldn't believe these people. He'd been terrified, and he still was, but Mia was his daughter and she would not be raised by these cold people.

Even if he made a thousand mistakes, which he knew he would, they would be made with love.

"She's a wonderful baby, but she's got an ear infection. She's sick and letting her cry probably did not help her ear."

The man huffed out his chest. "Well, it certainly wasn't good for *our* ears."

How had these people raised Skylar? Oh, wait, they hadn't. The nanny had. No wonder she was such a wild creature.

"If you want to see your granddaughter, we can set up a

supervised visitation," he said. "Just call me in advance and I'll meet you anywhere."

"Supervised visitation," Claire said. "She's our grand-daughter."

"And I'm her father," he said, knowing he would not leave his daughter alone with them until she was older. At this age, she was vulnerable and they would leave her with the help or someone they hired. Not happening.

The maid brought him the photo of Skylar that he asked for. "Thank you. She'll always know who her mother was. Who her family is. Now, I'm taking her home."

He walked out the door and his chest felt lighter than it had in two days. Tomorrow he would contact his lawyer and tell him to finalize that she belonged to him and he would need to know who her pediatrician was.

Even if Kayla wouldn't take him back, Mia was not going anywhere.

At the thought of Kayla, his chest ached. He had to find her.

"Come on, Mia, let's go find Kayla," he said as he buckled her into the car seat. "Daddy screwed up, but I'm going to try to make it right."

He could do this. He could be a much better father to her than her grandparents could ever be.

The sun was setting once they pulled out and headed toward Dallas. He glanced back to check on her and she had fallen asleep.

"Once we find Kayla, we're going home," he told her as he pulled out on the highway. Before he left to get Kayla, he'd googled a list of weekly hotels and one other place.

At the third extended-stay hotel on the edge of Fort Worth, he saw an Aston Martin car that looked just like hers.

Pulling up, he wondered how he was going to find which apartment she was in. Parking his truck, he took Mia out of her car seat and then went to the first apartment and knocked.

"Sorry, wrong apartment," he told the man who answered.

On the tenth try, she opened the door.

"Kayla," he said.

"Joshua," she said her eyes filling with tears. "Mia."

CHAPTER 26

ayla stood in the doorway in shock staring at Joshua, who had Mia in his arms.

"You got her back," she said.

"Yes, can we please come in and talk," he said.

As much as she wanted to, she could not accept the way he was now. It just couldn't happen.

"I'm not certain that's a good idea," she said. "I'm not taking you back after you acted the way you did."

The man sighed. "Please, Kayla, let me explain. Give me five minutes and then you can throw me and Mia out the door."

If she didn't do this, she would always wonder what he was going to say. She had to let him in.

"All right. Five minutes," she said.

When he walked in, he glanced at the computer she had set up on the table.

"You're using the new computer," he said.

"Yes," she replied. "Thank you."

He sank down on the loveseat and as much as she wanted to take Mia into her arms, she didn't. Once she touched the babe, she would agree to anything Joshua had to say. It was better not to hold her.

"Kayla, I'm a little slow at understanding people or myself, for that matter. When you walked out the door, I was shattered. The house became a death tomb with Eugenia giving me fits about letting you and the baby go. So I went out, just like you said I would, and I hated being at the club.

"The people seemed desperate. The same women, the same men, the music blaring so loud, you couldn't talk, I was miserable. I didn't belong there any longer and I knew it in less than an hour. I didn't even finish the beer I was drinking and walked out alone.

"That's not the life I want. You and Mia are who I want," he said softly. "You've changed me and made me a better man. A family man. Though God knows I'm terrified of hurting this child somehow."

Kayla started to cry. This was not what she was expecting. For him to admit that she had changed him had her hoping that maybe there was a chance.

"I went to the Beals to get Mia. On the way there, I realized what was bothering me about them. They remind me of my mother. No, I didn't have a nanny because Daddy would not allow her to hire one for me and my brothers. It was one of their greatest sources of conflict.

"I realized I was still acting just like my mother. In my quest to not get close to anyone, have a relationship, or get married, I became her. And by giving them Mia, I completed the cycle of doing what she would have done."

He'd understood. Thank goodness, he saw what he was doing and she didn't have to tell him. Thank goodness he'd gotten Mia back.

"When I went to get her, they were letting her cry herself to sleep," he said, running his hand through his hair. "I'm going to make mistakes. I'm going to screw up, but I now know for certain what I want. I want you, Kayla," he said.

He sank down to one knee and pulled a box out of his pocket. Balancing the baby on his knee, he fumbled a bit with the black velvet case.

"Kayla Scott, losing you, I realized how much I love you. How you make me a better man. A good man and I need you by my side, helping. Mia and I want to ask you to marry us. To join with us in creating a happy family. But more than anything, I want you to know you have my heart and my love, and I promise you that my wild and crazy womanizing days are behind me."

Kayla stared at him in shock. She couldn't believe he had come around.

She kneeled beside him and wrapped her arms around him. "I love you, Joshua. I have for days and you broke my heart when you let go of Mia. Promise me that we will work through any problems we have. That when you get scared, you'll come to me. When I get scared, I'll come to you and you'll help me. That no matter what, no one ever walks away again because I can't take it a second time."

"Always, sweetheart. Always. I know I screwed up and I'll do so again, but you tell me and we'll work it out."

"I love you, Joshua," she said, crying as they toppled to the floor. "Yes, I'll marry you."

"I love you, Kayla," he said, trying to keep Mia from getting crushed between them.

His mouth found hers and he kissed her thoroughly. When they broke apart, he turned to stare at her.

"The ring," she said. "Show me the ring."

He pulled out the box again and she gasped at the large emerald-cut diamond in the box.

"I got you the biggest one they had because I needed something to convince you to come back to me."

She laughed. "The ring is not what convinced me. You showing up here is what did the trick. Now we should get up off this floor. I think there is the outline of a dead body on the carpet."

Jumping up, he pulled her to standing. They sank down on the couch.

"Come here, Mia," she said.

The baby giggled and blew her a raspberry.

Tears filled her eyes. The foster child had finally found her own family and she loved both of these people more than she ever thought possible.

CHAPTER 27

*O*n their second Christmas together, Joshua glanced around at his family. This year they had added a couple of new additions. Samantha and Travis had a baby boy named Sam Travis after both his mother, Samantha, and his father.

Tanner and Emily's little boy arrived not long after Samuel and his name was Brandon Tanner after one of his Iraqi war heroes.

And Tucker and Kendra had a little girl that they named Nancy Rose after her sister. Three new babies and Mia who was now a year old.

His daughter wore a fancy Christmas dress that Kayla had bought her. For the last three days, Kayla had been sick and he was worried about her.

Their first wedding anniversary was coming up on January first and he wanted to get a sitter and take her to the fanciest restaurant in Fort Worth, celebrate with a night in a hotel, a wonderful dinner, and give her the best sex she'd ever had.

But if she was sick, he didn't know. Together they had made the decision to get pregnant since Mia was now a year old. Her first word had been *dada* and he thought his heart was going to melt in his chest when she cried out his name.

That was the sweetest word he had ever heard spoken.

Mia came running to him and she grasped her arms around his knees. His heart puddled as he hugged her tightly against him. Kayla walked toward him, a smile on her face. Hopefully, she was feeling better.

Last month, her business had made more money than she made at her old job and he was extremely proud of how she had created her own place. The Frantz Marketing company was laying off workers because they had lost so many clients and while Joshua hated that, Kayla had hired two of her coworkers to help her with her business. She promised to pay them well and they could work from home.

His wife reached his side. "Darling, I know why I've been sick."

"What's wrong," he said, hoping it was nothing major.

She pulled out a pregnancy stick. It showed the plus sign.

"I'm pregnant," she said. "Mia is going to have a brother or sister in August."

Speechless, he stared down at her and then he grinned. Lifting her into his arms, he kissed her while spinning her around.

Finally he set her down, realizing that might not be good for a pregnant woman. He hadn't been around Skylar when she was pregnant with Mia. But he planned on being by Kayla's side the entire time.

"Hey, everyone, great news," he said. "We're expecting." His family members raised their glasses and cheered. "I'm so thankful for you," he said, gazing at his wife.

"I love you, Joshua. You've made me whole," she said.

Mia held up her arms wanting to be included. "Me."

Joshua reached down and picked her up. This was his life. His family. And he felt blessed to have Kayla and Mia in his life and now a new baby.

One they would make mistakes with, but together they would learn. Together they could do anything.

They heard the old woman's cackle and knew Eugenia was among them.

"Jacob, I took a year off, but guess what. It's your turn. Who will you marry?"

His brother's blue eyes widened. "Oh, hell no, ghost. I'm not interested. Find someone else."

"That's what all you Burnett men say. And not a one of you has been able to stop me yet. Get ready, Jacob, it's your turn."

Jacob

PLEASE LEAVE A REVIEW

Thank you for reading Joshua and Kayla's story. This was not the story I was going to write, but it came to me and I loved the idea of a bachelor who has a baby thrown into his life. A baby that's his. I hope you enjoyed seeing him learn what was important in life.

Did you enjoy the book? Reviews help authors. I would appreciate you posting a review at your favorite retailer.

Follow Sylvia McDaniel on Facebook.

Sign up for my New Book Alert and receive a complimentary book and also freebies and discounted books!

I'LL BE HOME FOR CHRISTMAS

*a*s Olivia Miller drove along the highway, the night hurled snow like Mother Nature spewed the white stuff.

The blizzard warnings were right. The wind howled, blowing her little hatchback all over the road while big flakes smacked the windshield like tiny snowballs. What was she doing out in this mess?

Music blared on the radio, and Olivia cringed at the Christmas carol that filled her car, asking for presents, snow, and mistletoe. Mother Nature was delivering on the snow.

"I'll be in Hell for Christmas," she sang changing the words, tears flowing down her cheeks as she thought about her miserable life.

This day couldn't get much worse.

The holiday season was supposed to be a beautiful, happy time. A time of love and family, and damn it, this was going to be the worst Christmas ever.

Trying to watch the road, she wiped at the tears that had

not stopped flowing since she'd left Billings. She'd waited until the last minute to leave, waiting around for the big jerk since he promised to go with her. And now she was on the road to Whitefish later than she planned. The storm they'd been predicting was upon her. In the dark, she watched as the snowflakes flew in the headlights, the wind shoving from lane to lane, her windshield wipers working overtime to remove snow.

Her sleigh was struggling and she wasn't feeling jolly, merry, or bright.

For the first time in years, her mother had issued a demand that the family gather at Christmastime for an important announcement and she'd thought that she and the jerk would be the center of that revelation.

In her mind, she'd dreamed of an engagement ring and a happily ever after with him asking her in front of her family. Only the dream was a nightmare, and she'd been the only one thinking of a pledge to marry. Not the big jerk.

The only disclosure she'd be making would be that she was still single and alone. That the man she'd thought was Mr. Right was actually Mr. All Wrong. Mr. All Wrong caught in bed with his coworker. Even now her eyes had a hard time unseeing the two of them entwined together, naked.

And then there was a second life-changing event that had come completely out of the blue taking her by surprise.

The only thing that could be worse would be if she was pregnant. Thank goodness she'd been on the pill. Especially now.

Somewhere her life had taken a wrong turn and she'd found herself on a road she didn't know how to navigate.

Until today, she'd thought that everything was going great. Then life imploded and everything that could go wrong, did, including the job she loved.

Fired.

So what was the family message if not her engagement? She'd not been home since she graduated from college. Time seemed to have gotten away from her and she'd been focused on the asshole and being the best at her career.

So much for the job and the man she loved.

This was not the first time she'd found a boyfriend cheating on her. What was wrong with her that she seemed to choose men who couldn't keep their dick in their pants?

With a sigh, she wondered how her sisters would react to the news that, once again, she was on her own. Once again, she'd caught her man in bed with someone else. She doubted her siblings ever had problems in regard to men. Especially Amelia, the golden girl.

One of the reasons she avoided going home was she knew she'd have to deal with her sisters. Why the urgency for the family to spend Christmas together? They'd grown up, and once they reached college, had become disconnected. By choice.

And now the twins would be there. The favored girls. No, not the oldest woman but two girls that could do no wrong. Amelia's life was always perfect. Head cheerleader, valedictorian, Mensa member, and scholarship winner.

Now a lawyer.

The family super achiever who probably had never broken a nail and her hair and makeup were always perfect and the world awaited her like a queen with her subjects. Bow down to Her Highness.

And Emma was a carbon copy, though she was the introverted twin. Still a super achiever, Emma kept her accomplishments more on the down-low compared to Amelia's shouting from the rooftops. A nurse in the NICU unit, she helped to save babies.

Olivia...she just plodded along, thinking everything was fine and then she discovered the truth. And nothing was right. None of her decisions, her career, everything gone to hell.

No one would ever call her an overachiever. And she doubted her sisters had ever been fired from their jobs.

The snow was beginning to pile up on the road and the few cars that had been on the highway suddenly disappeared. It was just her and a truck that had been behind her for the last several miles. When she reached the next town, she would find a hotel and spend the night.

Waiting for the big ass had been a huge mistake and now she was paying the price in more ways than one. Not only had he cheated on her, but he'd put her so far behind schedule to return home. The plan had been to leave at noon. At five, she gave up and went to his apartment. Mistake number two.

At this rate, she wouldn't make it home tonight. And maybe that was for the best. And yet she needed her mother's hug. It was the reason she'd not completely canceled.

Maybe the two of them could figure out where she'd gone wrong. And there was this supposed family announcement that her mother wanted everyone to hear.

In the white glare of her headlights, her brain realized an elk stood in the middle of the road like the king of the mountains. His size was intimidating and no match for her little car. The damn animal was staring her down, not moving. Her foot immediately moved to the brakes and when she hit them, her car began to spin on the snowy road.

Mistake number three. Don't slam on the brakes on ice and snow.

With a scream, she turned the wheel in the opposite direction and when she finally gained control, she saw the snow bank just as her car slammed into it.

Maybe this day could get worse. Her head smashed into the driver's door window and blackness came rushing toward her. Why had she waited on the big jerk? Why?

Available Everywhere

CUPID STUPID

Cupid, Texas

"Valentine's Day. Today is the cheating snake's wedding day," Taylor Braxton said, flipping her blonde hair over her shoulder before taking a sip of wine. Her third glass of the evening. "I'd like to propose a toast to his new wife. May she never find him in her bed with someone else, like I found her in mine."

The three women clinked glasses.

"Maybe it was for the best. After all, lawmen are known for being serial cheaters," Meghan, one of Taylor's best friends, said in her quiet librarian voice. She gave a shake of auburn hair, her emerald eyes filled with sympathy.

Still the same after all these years, Taylor wondered if Meghan ever raised her voice even during a climax. Did she scream with passion, or just say oh? And Taylor never wanted to know the answer to that question.

Yes, lawmen were not the exception to cheating. Many men were sleaze bags who thought infidelity was nothing.

Kelsey, Taylor's other best friend leaned in close. "Well, if you hadn't found him locked in the arms of another woman, you wouldn't have come back to Cupid."

"True," Taylor agreed.

Pushing her dark brunette hair back over her shoulder, Kelsey smiled. "I can't believe we're all here together again. Just like the old days when we were young and naive and so vulnerable. Now, we're all grown up and--"

"Still single," Meghan said with a sigh.

"Yep, no eligible man on my radar," Kelsey admitted. "Who would want to date a woman with three pain in the ass brothers watching over her?"

Kelsey's announcement surprised Taylor. Of the three of them, Kelsey was who she thought would walk down the aisle first. Instead, not one of them was wearing a ring, and frankly, she found it odd she'd come the closest to a honeymoon.

"I don't want a man. I'm giving up. I'm going to remain single the rest of my life," Taylor announced.

After her last attempt at love, the time to step away had arrived in the form of a revealed booty call. Now, her focus on the family business was the most important thing in her life.

"Oh yeah, that's the life I want," Meghan replied, sarcasm dripping in her tone. "Always the third wheel when you're around couples. Every holiday your relatives asking if there is something wrong with you or have you tried online dating. Blind dates with your next-door neighbor's son, who is so kind that he still lives with his mother." She shivered. "No, thanks."

Meghan's appearance fitted the sweet, innocent librarian

image, but her tongue was sharp and precise. Sometimes even Taylor was shocked at what came out of her smart mouth.

Setting her wine glass down on the table Kelsey leaned forward. "Or your brothers' glancing at every man you bring home like he's a terrorist, and should they learn he's sleeping with their sister, he would wake up six feet under." Kelsey giggled. "They don't know, but I lost my virginity the first semester of college during pledge week."

"Ohh...with someone you cared about?" Taylor asked.

She sighed. "Not really. We were two virgins who wanted to rid ourselves of the stigma. A fumbling, truly awful, awkward experience. After that horrible first time, I concentrated on my studies and not on men."

"What about you, Taylor? When did you lose your virginity?" Meghan asked.

"Prom night," she said, shaking her head. "Billy Ray Smith."

"Oh my gosh, he's married and living one town over."

"Thank God. He was mistake number one. I was young and foolish." And oh, so stupid, she thought.

That night he'd convinced her everyone was doing the nasty and if she didn't give it up, she would be the only virgin left in school. Curious about the forbidden fruit and wanting to fit in, she listened to him.

Meghan laughed. "Well, we certainly know who popped my cherry. Max Vandenberg, football superstar jerk."

The three women sighed. Kelsey shifted uneasily in her chair. "We thought we were going to change the world."

Taylor snickered. "I think the world changed us."

Meghan giggled. "Remember that silly superstition from high school?"

"Which one? There were several," Kelsey said. "I especially liked the one where the football boys had to put a pair of girl's panties on the top of the goal post if they wanted a winning season."

So many things happened in a small town where gridiron was king. The football team could get away with so much more than the other school sports.

"While the drill team practiced in our uniforms, all our undies were stolen from the girls' gym. I remember going commando, like, yesterday." Taylor chuckled.

Kelsey turned toward her. "Max Vandenberg was the panty thief. Did you hear that he played professional football for the Dallas Cowboys for a while?"

"Until he got hurt. Now he's back." Meghan shook her head. "Right back here under my nose - the big jerk. He's coaching at my school."

"Why does it seem like many of our classmates left and eventually returned."

"Yes, Ryan Jones is back. My brother told me he's sheriff now," Kelsey said, drinking another glass of vino. "He was my ex. So two exes back in town and another one's married and lives nearby."

"I don't consider Billy Ray an ex."

Sure, Taylor lost her virginity the night of prom, but recognized she would never marry Billy Ray. *Redneck* was a polite term for that kid. The ex that crushed her was in Dallas where he belonged with his skanky new wife.

Sitting there, she glanced at her besties from grade school.

"Wonder how many girls fell for that Cupid superstition? Did you guys ever do that one?" Taylor asked.

"Oh no," Meghan said. "I didn't like getting undressed in gym class."

"Oh no," Kelsey echoed. "If my brothers caught me dancing naked around the statue in the town square, I would have been sealed away in a nunnery until my female parts shriveled. What about you?"

"No," she said, thinking she didn't believe that nonsense.

Taylor looked at the two women sitting at the table. She poured the last of the second bottle of wine. The music seemed louder, the laughter shriller, and yet she was having so much fun, she didn't want to stop. Tomorrow she'd probably regret the amount of alcohol they were consuming, but tonight felt good. Old friends, memories, and alcohol helping her forget the importance of this damn day.

"You remember when all the cheerleaders did the naked Cupid dance, all hoping to find their true love. How did the magic work out for them?" Kelsey said with a laugh.

Taylor shook her head. "I remember. The football team showed up unexpectedly with cameras in hand and when the squad returned to school they faced suspension."

The principal decided to make them examples.

Meghan frowned and gazed at the women, her blue eyes large, her expression one of disgust. "Don't feel too badly for them. They're all married. In fact, most of them have babies. If the superstition is true, it worked very well for them. What the hell is wrong with us?"

Taylor threw her hands up. "I'm not looking to get married. Right now, my focus is my parents' restaurant. I don't need a man."

After her disastrous engagement, the time had come to put

the idea of marriage and children and happily ever after on the shelf.

Turning in her chair, Meghan looked at Kelsey. "What about you? Do you want to marry?"

Kelsey leaned on her hands. "Yes, I would like to find a man, but my brothers run them off faster than a deer during hunting season. So I'll be working on the boutique I'm preparing to open for business. One year is all I have to make a profit. Or I'll be moving back to the city. What about you, Meghan?"

She tossed back her hair and stared them straight in the eye. "I'm twenty-five years old. I'm ready. My ovaries are beginning to shrivel like a prune. Bring on the right man and I'll race him to the altar."

The idea hit Taylor smack in the stomach, and while it seemed preposterous, the idea was too good to pass up. She shook her head at the two of them, giggling. "Then let's do it."

Frowns appeared on their faces as they stared at her. "What?"

She checked her watch. "It worked for all those other women. Why not us? The superstition says at midnight anyone chanting and dancing naked around the fountain will soon meet their true love. I've never believed in the notion, but hey, I'm game. We've got thirty minutes. Let's go kick some Cupid butt and see if that superstition is real or not."

Meghan's eyes widened. "You want me to take off my clothes and dance in front of you and everyone else in town, chanting some silly verse?"

"Oh, most people will be asleep and I've seen you *au naturel* before. I'll be too busy dancing to notice you and your jiggling tatas."

Laughing, Kelsey gazed at Taylor. "And you think this is going to work."

No, she didn't believe in superstitions. She walked under ladders, stepped on cracks, and black cats didn't frighten her. Friday the thirteenth was just another day and dancing without clothes around a statue wasn't going to land her a husband.

She didn't want or need a man in her life. But she'd do this for her friends.

"We're late bloomers. Everyone else did this in high school. We never had the courage, but now we're older, some of us desperate. Let's do it."

Kelsey lifted her glass and drained the alcohol. "I'm in. What about you, Meghan?"

"Oh, it's starting again. During high school, you girls could get me into more trouble. You're back in town less than twenty-four hours and already you're plotting mischief."

"Oh, come on, it'll be fun," Taylor said, downing the last of her drink and signaling the waitress.

"The temperature outside is colder than a well digger - and we're getting naked," Meghan whined. "Tonight, other women are being wined and dined and we're going to dance without our clothes, in the town square? Something is wrong with this picture."

"Think of the thrill. The tales you can tell your children," Taylor said, the adventure of doing something dangerous sending a ripple of excitement through her. Years had passed since her last prank and this was the kind of stunt that got her juices flowing.

"Daring." Kelsey grabbed her purse. "I haven't done anything like this since college. I'm just drunk enough my logical, rational side is being held hostage by my fun side."

"Are you in?" Taylor asked not certain Meghan would agree.

With a sigh Meghan finished her wine. "I don't want to be the only old maid. Of course, I'm in."

Available Everywhere!

Contemporary Romance
Burnett Brides Contemporary Times
Travis

Tanner

Tucker

Joshua

Jacob

Justin

Cameron

Caleb

Cody

Desiree

Burnett Brides Contemporary Box Set Books 5-7

Burnett Brides Contemporary Box Set 8-10

Burnett Brides Contemporary Box Set 11-14

Return to Cupid, Texas
Cupid Stupid

Cupid Scores

Cupid's Dance

Cupid Help Me!

Cupid Cures

**Cupid's Heart

Cupid Santa

**Cupid Second Chance

Cupid Charmer

Cupid Crazy

Cupid's Bachelorette

Cupid Games

Return to Cupid Box Set Books 1-3
Cupid Help Me Box Set Books 4-6
Return to Cupid Box Set Books 7-9
Return to Cupid Box Set Books 10-12
**The Unlucky Bride

Contemporary Romance
My Sister's Boyfriend
The Wanted Bride
The Reluctant Santa
The Relationship Coach
Secrets, Lies, & Online Dating

Bride, Texas Multi-Author Series
**The Unlucky Bride

Coming Home for Christmas
I'll Be Home for Christmas
White Christmas
Santa's Baby
All I Want For Christmas
Box Set

Inheriting An Irish Groom
Inheriting a Scottish Castle

Kissing Oaks Billionaire Brothers
The Cowboy Billionaire's Lucky Break
The Cowboy Billionaire's Fate
The Cowboy Billionaire's Playbook

The Cowboy Billionaire's Secret
The Cowboy Billionaire's Deception
The Cowboy Billionaire's Match
Kissing Oaks Billionaire Brothers Box Set 1-3
Kissing Oaks Billionaire Brothers Box Set 4-6

Lipstick and Lead 2.0
Nailing the Hit Man
Nailing the Billionaire
Nailing the Single Dad
Box Set

Secrets of Mustang Island
Secrets of a Summer Place
Secrets of a Runaway Bride
Secrets From the Past
Secrets of a Reckless Life
Secrets of a Hidden Life
Secrets of a Midnight Letter

Secrets of Mustang Island Novellas
The Summer I Loved You
When We Meet Again
Christmas at Mustang Island

The Langley Legacy
Collin's Challenge

Short Sexy Reads
Racy Reunions Series

Paying For the Past
My Christmas Soldier
Cupid's Revenge

Western Historicals
A Hero's Heart
Second Chance Cowboy
Ethan

American Brides
**Katie: Bride of Virginia

Angel Creek Christmas Brides
**Charity
**Ginger
**Minne
**Cora
Angel Creek Christmas Box Set

Bad Girls of the West
Scandalous Sadie
Ravenous Rose
Tempting Tessa
Nellie's Redemption
Bad Girls Box Set

The Burnett Brides Series
The Rancher Takes A Bride
The Outlaw Takes A Bride
The Marshal Takes A Bride

The Christmas Bride
Boxed Set

Lipstick and Lead Series
Desperate
Deadly
Dangerous
Daring
Determined
Deceived
Defiant
Devious
Lipstick and Lead Box Set Books 1-4
Lipstick and Lead Box Set Books 5-9
Lipstick and Lead Box Set Books 1-9
**Quinlan's Quest

Mail Order Bride Tales
**A Brother's Betrayal
**Pearl
**Ace's Bride

Scandalous Suffragettes of the West
**Abigail
Bella
Mistletoe Scandal

Southern Historical Romance
A Scarlet Bride

The Cuvier Women
Wronged
Betrayed
Beguiled
Boxed Set

The Debutante's of Durango
The Debutante's Scandal
The Debutante's Gamble
The Debutante's Revenge
The Debutante's Santa
Box Set

** Denotes a sweet book.

**Want to learn about my new releases before anyone else?
Sign up for my New Book Alert and receive a
complimentary book.**

Sylvia McDaniel is a USA Today Bestselling author with over one hundred western historical and contemporary romance novels under her belt. Known for creating memorable bad boys and good girls who can't help getting into trouble, she spends her days weaving compelling tales filled with heart, humor, and unexpected plot twists. Her family-oriented stories have earned her a loyal fanbase, and she's always dreaming up new ways to keep her readers turning the page.

Married to her best friend for over thirty years, Sylvia lives in Colorado, where she enjoys hiking and taking in the natural beauty of the forest that borders their home. Their spoiled dachshund, Zeus (who has his own column in her newsletter), and brat dog Bailey keeps them company on their adventures.

Sylvia keeps close ties to her southern roots, especially when it comes to football. A dedicated fan of both the Denver Broncos and the Dallas Cowboys, she's happiest when they're winning.

Love books? Love deals? Love a little mischief? Sign up for my Substack—it's free!
https://sylviamcdanielauthor.substack.com/
The End

www.ingramcontent.com/pod-product-compliance
Lightning Source LLC
Chambersburg PA
CBHW051434170626
46809CB00006B/2453